BLACK LACE AND BULLETS

Published by

www.GeniePub.com

A NOVEL BY **BOB RILEY**

BLACK LACE AND BULLETS

– First Edition –

GENIE PUBLISHING
www.GeniePub.com

Author: Bob Riley

ISBN: 978-1-889137-66-7

Category: Mystery / Intrigue / Irish / Female Protagonist

Printed in the United States of America

ACKNOWLEDGMENTS

I take full responsibility for all 50,000 words transferred from my imagination, one finger punch at a time, to my computer. That process could have been terminated any number of times if it hadn't been for encouragement rendered by friends and relatives. Sometimes, these can be the same. Frank and Cally were the first to recognize greatness and continued to provide encouragement. Ann was coerced into reading changes and rereading corrections, always providing positive feedback. My son, Keith, painstakingly went through the whole manuscript editing it. My granddaughter, Aurelia, a professional model, willingly posed for hours waiting for me to find the "right shot". My grandson, Joseph, put his many talents to work in designing the cover. I asked and received guidance from MaryBeth, however, decisions on what I used were mine. I am sure there were others that made contributions and my sincerest appreciation to all of you.

Also, to my publisher, for her many suggestions and her patience, my sincerest thanks.

The seed for this project started with my second wife, Virginia. She was a great writer, well versed in the use of the English language. She always wanted to write a novel. Her problem was she couldn't come up with a plot. We decided to collaborate, I ran a couple of possible plots by her, for various reasons, none were acceptable. We ran out of time.

Occasionally, when I can't sleep, I'll make up a story, sometimes, it puts me asleep, other times it keeps me awake. This time it was about hiding a prince by disguising him as a girl. That is not the story in this book, but it was a starting point. The rest just evolved, so Virginia, here it is, my feeble attempt to complete our dream.

Dedicated with love,
Bob

BLACK LACE AND BULLETS

TABLE OF CONTENTS

Chapter One

IRELAND, 1740

Terrance N. Thomas stood in front of his thatched-roof house looking out over his farm, now brown with winter colors. The year was 1745; it was becoming increasingly more difficult being Catholic in Ireland. He wondered how long his family could maintain their ownership of the farm that had been in the family for generations. He had thought often of leaving Ireland and going somewhere he could raise his family and practice his religion. He had discussed it with his family, but his love for the land and his optimism that things would improve prevented him from making a decision. His family included his wife, Mary Elizabeth, a daughter, Kathleen, and two sons, Terry Jr., seventeen, and Timmy, fifteen. Kathleen had just married a farmer from the south of Ireland and had only recently moved there. His sons had grown into very capable farmers, if only the government would let them just be farmers.

They had barely survived the great freeze in 1740. With the weather cooperating, the farm had had two very good years, and this season looked fine. The two boys were on the roof of the barn making repairs when their father came out of the barn leading the horse. The horse, Ed, was harnessed and dragging the chain used to pull tree stumps out of the ground. They had recently cut down two big trees that were dying. They had dug around the roots to get them ready to be removed. Now it only remained to pull them out.

Terry Jr. hollered down asking if his father wanted their help.

"No, thanks. Ed and I can do it. We need that roof finished before it rains," their father said. With that, he and Ed went over the hill and out of view.

It was several hours later when the boys broke for dinner. When they got to the house their mother asked where their father was.

"He went to pull stumps, should be back by now," said Terry.

His mother replied, "Terry, go see what's keeping him. Tell him dinner is getting cold."

Terry grabbed his hat and took off to where the tree stumps were. He saw Ed standing there, but did not see his father. When he got closer he saw his father lying on the ground. He rushed to him and saw that he was unconscious and bleeding. He ran back to the house to get his mother. She sent Timmy to get the doctor and returned with Terry to her husband. She had brought some sheets and a blanket. She slowly rolled him onto his back and put the blanket over him. After cleaning his face, she looked for any wounds, finding only cuts on his head. As she was applying bandages to his head, the doctor arrived. He quickly examined him and said, "Let's get him into the house."

They put him on the bed and covered him with a quilt. The doctor cleaned and bandaged the wounds and said that Mr. Thomas had serious injuries to his head. He gave her some medicine for pain if he woke up. As he left, the doctor said, "Now it's up to God." Mary Elizabeth and her two sons knelt beside the bed and prayed.

Mary Elizabeth spent the night sitting beside her husband holding his hand. The two boys either sat before the fire in the main room or replaced their mother sitting beside their father. They kept a hot pot of tea for their mother when she came to sit in her rocker near the fire. About five in the morning, their mother came to the door of her bedroom and said, "Come in, boys. God has made his decision and has taken your father." The three of them once again knelt beside the bed and prayed.

The mother said, "Timmy, go tell Mrs. O'Donnell and she'll notify the others. Then go tell Father Murphy."

Mrs. O'Donnell and several other women of the neighborhood arrived in a very short time. Mrs. O'Donnell took charge, and she and the other women started to prepare Mr. Thomas's body, first washing him and then giving him a clean shave. Then they clothed him in a shroud, and placed a crucifix on his chest and a rosary in his hand. The bed had been stripped and covered with clean sheets. Here he would lie for the wake. Candles were placed around the body, and clay pipes and tobacco were set out around the room. A plate of snuff was placed where all could take a pinch. The clocks were stopped and the mirrors were covered or turned around facing the wall. Three chairs were placed beside the bed for the mourners known as keeners.

The Caointhe, the lead keener, was a cousin; the other two were close friends. Their sounds of mourning and prayers were heard throughout the house. Mary Elizabeth joined them for a while and then left to prepare the other part of the wake.

She would mourn for a long time, but now she would celebrate the love and joy Terry had brought to her, their children, and all who knew him.

She went to the cellar and got the three jugs of whiskey Terry had put there. One was his special, a jug of fine, aged whiskey, and the others were for friendly drinking. She took them upstairs and put the good stuff away for a toast. The other two she put on a table, which the neighbors were filling with food. When all her neighbors, friends, and relatives had arrived and paid their respects, she got their attention and filled glasses with the good stuff and passed them around.

When all had a glass, she held hers up and said, "A toast to Terrence N. Thomas, a loving husband and father, a true and loyal friend, a man who leaves this world better because he was here. He is now with our Lord." She raised her glass, and as the room was filled with shouts of "Terrance" she downed her drink.

She looked toward the musician and said, "Let's celebrate Terry's love of life and his love of good times with friends. Please play, fellows."

The celebration began and lasted until midnight. At that time, Father Murphy led them in the Rosary. Most of the people left, but a few close friends stayed far into the night swapping stories about Terry.

Chapter Two

THE DECISION

The next two years were good years: the weather cooperated and there were two good crops. It was during the fall of the second year that Mary Elizabeth fell ill to influenza and passed away. She was laid to rest beside her husband in the cemetery next to the church.

Terry had been courting a neighbor girl, Molly O'Reilly, and planned on getting married soon. They received a good offer for the farm, and the two boys decided to go to the colonies and begin a new life. Terry and Molly would be married before their departure. They began getting things ready for the move; they started making plans and found others in the area also planning to make the journey to the colonies.

Arrangements were made to meet, get acquainted, and decide on a course of action. They made plans to contact an agency which could locate land for them and help them find and book passage on a ship. Once they found the date the ship was sailing, they began preparing for the trip. Space was at a premium on the boat. They would be limited to a small sack of belongings. Anything of value they would sell and turn into gold.

Their sister, Kathleen, would come up and help them get rid of everything. They would load up what Kathleen wanted and would drive south to Kathy's farm. The trip would take almost a month.

As they traveled, they would sell various items on the wagon. When they arrived at Kathy's house, they would sell anything that was left. Then they would sell the horses and wagon and make their way to Cork, where they would board their ship.

Chapter Three

THE COLONIES

T he *Hannah*, scheduled to sail on April 6, was a solidly built sailing ship, unlike the ones used a hundred years later to transport those fleeing the great famine. During those voyages, it was estimated that 20 percent of the travelers would die.

The three boarded the ship in Cork, each assigned a small bunk; no privacy and no comfort, but still it felt great to finally to be on their way. The *Hannah* had a very fortunate trip: good weather and favorable winds resulted in a trip of only five weeks, arriving in Boston in early May. Once in Boston, they joined with another group to make up a wagon train going to western Pennsylvania. Each family had to buy what they would need for at least a year.

Tim and Terry each bought a wagon, a team of oxen, and a cow. Each purchased a good rifle, powder and shot, plus all the other provisions they would need. The wagon train formed up and was ready to leave by the second week in May, giving the group enough time to get there and prepare for settling in before the winter. They had selected land bordering the Dell River in western Pennsylvania, each receiving about 60 acres. Terry and Timmy had side-by-side acreage along the river and immediately began clearing a common area on their property. They decided to build a log cabin and share it, at least through the winter.

First they had to cut and trim all the trees to be used for the cabins, and remove the stumps. They prepared the cleared area for a garden and helped Molly get it planted. After that it would be her responsibility.

With the garden planted, they began to build a two-room log cabin. Neighbors helped with the initial construction. Occasionally Tim and Terry would help a neighbor remove tree stumps or carry out some construction requiring additional manpower. The settlement was taking shape and should be ready for the winter that was approaching.

Timmy had been courting a young neighbor girl, Beth O'Dow. She would be sixteen in October; her father wouldn't let her marry until then. As summer passed, the garden grew and they made good progress on the house. By October 1, they had the roof on and most of the caulking done. Terry had built a large fireplace in the living section, to be used for cooking and heating. They decided to have a combined housewarming and a wedding to celebrate their new home. There would be a visiting priest in the settlement during the second week in October; thus the party and the wedding were scheduled for October 12. It was to be a settlement occasion.

The entire community got caught up in preparing for the celebration. The brothers decided to put in a wooden floor to facilitate dancing, just in case the weather didn't cooperate. It would be the only cabin in the area with a wooden floor.

On the day of the wedding, a mild fall day, the sky was filled with sunshine illuminating all the multicolored trees in the surrounding forest. The air was filled with the smell of venison being barbecued on a spit. Tables were being set in anticipation of the mounds of food now being prepared for the feast.

Father Mike had a busy week, hearing confessions and performing four baptisms, one funeral, and three weddings. Two of the weddings were performed earlier; all would be celebrated here. A piper in traditional Irish garb was stationed at the edge of the clearing and piped the guests in. An excited and cheerful group it was. They felt they had worked hard and were ready for the winter ahead, and were definitely ready for a celebration.

At the appointed hour, Timmy and Beth were joined in marriage by Father Mike. They performed the traditional "tying the knot," using a bright green ribbon.

Giving the Irish toast, Timmy and Beth turned to the guests and said, "Friends and relatives, so fond and dear, 'tis our greatest pleasure to have you here. When many years this day has passed, fondest memories will always last. So we drink a cup of Irish mead and ask God's blessing in your hour of need."

The crowd raised their glasses and responded, "On this special day, our wish to you, the goodness of the old, the best of the new. God bless you both who drink this mead, may it always fill your need."

The community had carried a supply of Irish whiskey for special occasions, such as toasting newlyweds. After the toast, they settled down to celebrating with local corn whiskey from the O'Riley still. Not as tasty as Irish, but just as potent. Many would wake up the next day with an aching head.

Terry and Molly had moved into the cabin several weeks before the wedding. The sleeping area was one large room, divided by hanging blankets, giving visual privacy. Although sounds were muffled, they were not blocked. On the night of the wedding, Terry and Molly moved in beside the fireplace to spend the night, giving the newlyweds some privacy. After five weeks on board the *Hannah*, they were used to mentally shutting out sounds, so on the next day, they would move back to their sleeping area.

The winter passed and the settlement prospered.

Chapter Four

THE CLAN MOVES WEST

Terry and Timmy continued to clear the land, and they raised families. Each generation would acquire more land. By the third generation, the clan was cultivating more than a thousand acres. There were plenty of Thomases around, but the clan now included other names, mostly Irish, as the daughters married and had families. The clan, instilled with the pioneering spirit of Terry and Timmy, would keep moving west, leaving vibrant communities behind. There are communities in Pennsylvania, Ohio, Illinois, Kansas, and finally Idaho, with descendants of Terry and Timmy.

In Idaho, the Thomas farm had grown into a huge corporation owned by various branches of the Thomas family. Most were farmers raising Idaho potatoes. Others were merchants associated with selling farm items. There were also professionals, such as doctors, lawyers, engineers, and others needed to support a community. Go back far enough and most were related. In every generation, there was a Terry and a Timothy.

Chapter Five

TERRY THOMAS

Terry Thomas, born and raised in Idaho, graduated from Texas A&M with a degree in mechanical engineering and was commissioned as a second lieutenant in the US Marine Corps Reserve. After graduation, he married his high school sweetheart, Erin O'Malley. A week after their first anniversary, she gave birth to Kathleen, starting another generation of Thomas's. Two years later Timmy was born.

Terry managed the maintenance department on the farm. He had built a house for his family and enjoyed his work. His job involved him in many projects on the farm's buildings, houses, barns, and other structures. He also was involved in supervising the maintenance facility, a large building where upkeep was performed on all the farm equipment.

A week after Pearl Harbor, Terry received a notice advising him to report to the Marine Corps training center in San Diego for training with the newly formed 29th Special Engineering Group. He had been promoted to captain. The group would be trained as specialists in destroying anything that prevented the Marines from completing their mission, be it on land or sea. They performed their mission from Guadalcanal to Okinawa, participating in all major landings. The unit was in Australia, training for the invasion of Japan, when the US dropped the atom bomb and Japan surrendered.

Terry, now a lieutenant colonel, had received three Purple Hearts, two Bronze Stars, and one Silver Star, and had been recommended for the Navy Cross. He was now the commander of the Group.

The Group was about to be shipped home, except for a few who had recently arrived and did not have enough points to go home. As Terry stood in front of the formation of five hundred, he mentally reminisced: of the five hundred who had been in the original group, only twenty-seven were still here. The unit was diminished with the KIAs, the MIAs, the WIAs, and the POWs. There were also those who were transferred to other groups. As he thought of those gone, he choked up and his eyes watered; he was just able to command, "Pass in review." The next day, he led the group onto a naval transport for the trip home – not a luxury cruise, but a relaxed one with no worry about enemy subs or aircrafts.

At the decommissioning formation in San Diego, Terry was presented with the Navy Cross. He was separated and took the train back to Idaho to a hero's welcome. The whole clan and many others were there to greet him, but his eyes were for Erin and the kids. His job was waiting for him.

He was now in charge of all maintenance on the farm. This included a very large heavy-equipment maintenance shop, a general vehicle garage for trucks and cars, an electrical shop, and a plumbing shop. He had a nice house and plans for a new, larger one – yet he was restless. Maybe his time in the Marines was having an effect. Regardless of the reason, he decided he wanted to leave and go out on his own. The decision made, he sold his house and half of his stock in the farm back to the corporation. With his savings from his time in the Marines, he had over $200,000. His remaining stock would provide him with about $200 a month, enough to survive without touching his savings.

He bought a new truck and a small travel trailer, loaded up the kids and all their possessions, and headed south. They hit Las Vegas, the Grand Canyon, and New Orleans and kept going. They drove into the Florida panhandle and visited Pensacola. They drove to Orlando, still a sleepy Florida town, where Disney World was just Walt's dream. They headed over to Daytona and drove on the beach and the kids played in the ocean. They got on US 1 and started toward Key West. The east coast of Florida was just starting to boom. When they reached Miami, Terry decided this was an area where he wanted to stay. He started looking around and pricing real estate. He found what he wanted fifteen miles south of Miami. He bought five hundred acres on the west side of US 1 and fifty acres between US 1 and the ocean.

He picked twenty acres at the south end of his property on the west side of US 1 and began to build their house. He contracted out the concrete work and found another independent contractor willing to help him. Together they built the entire house: framing, plumbing, wiring, roofing, and finishing. They had worked well together and decided that they would start their own construction company, "Thomas and Waterbury." They contracted for custom-built homes going up in established neighborhoods.

The business thrived, and they decided to build their own community on two hundred acres of land that Terry owned. Terry laid out the development and began putting in the required utilities and roads. They created two lakes; one they called Lake Thomas and the other Lake Waterbury. Around the lakes they built two communities, upscale homes around Lake Waterbury and more modest homes around Lake Thomas. The project was a success from the beginning, and the partners began thinking about their next project, a shopping mall. They bought another hundred acres of Terry's property. The company had done well and made both partners wealthy.

Terry's kids, Kathy and Timmy, were now in high school. Timmy was in his second year, and Kathy was a senior. Kathy had been accepted by a college in Maine, and Timmy had applied to Georgia Tech.

* * *

Timmy worked part-time for his father's company, starting as the lowest laborer and becoming a qualified carpenter and an adequate electrician. This year, Timmy planned to take the summer off and work on their beach house located just across the highway from their house. Timmy's father had built the original structure that was little more than a bathhouse. Timmy planned on adding a fireplace, a kitchen, a second-floor loft, and two bedrooms downstairs. When needed, he would get help from the company. If he had enough time, he would put in a patio and a barbecue.

He worked all summer with numerous interruptions from Kathy's friend, who was there almost the entire time. He would take a lunch break and go to the beach for a swim and have his lunch. The girls thought it was enormously funny to lie facedown, topless, when Timmy was there.

One day, when there was four girls lying in the aforementioned position, Timmy took a bucket of ice water and, running between the girls lying on their beach towels, poured the ice water on their backs. There were high-pitched screams as the girl jumped up leaving their bras behind. When they became aware of their situation, they looked up to see Timmy standing there looking at them and taking pictures. They covered their breasts with their hands and tried to reach down to pick up their tops. The screaming continued as they tried to hold up their tops and chase Timmy. As they chased him, he yelled back, "See you in the funny papers." He didn't show up the next day.

On Monday afternoon, Timmy received a call that his father had been in an accident and was in serious condition. By the time Timmy and Kathy arrived at the hospital, their mother was there and waiting for them. "He fell from the fourth floor of the new building. He is surgery right now, but the doctor says it doesn't look good," she said.

His father succumbed to his injury the following week. A traditional wake was held, and he was cremated. His ashes now rested on the mantel in his den, and Timmy's mother would eventually decide where they would be placed.

George Waterbury, Timmy's father's partner, continued to manage the company. As is normal in a small private company, they had an insurance policy whereby if one partner died, the other partner would become the sole owner, and the deceased's heirs would receive an amount of money consistent with the value of the company.

Trusts were set up for Kathy and Timmy in the amount of several millions each. It was to be theirs when they became twenty-one or graduated from college, whichever occurred first. Money would be provided for college and living expenses. There was still land, which would be sold to Mr. Waterbury when he needed it. This did not include the twenty acres their house occupied or the fifty acres across the highway on the ocean. Financially, the family was in excellent shape.

Kathy had gotten her BA degree and was in her second year of graduate school, and Timmy was ready to graduate college, when their mother passed away. She was cremated, and her ashes joined her husband's in the den. The decision was made to wait until Timmy and Kathy settled down before deciding on the ashes' final resting place. They decided that Kathy would take the homestead and Timmy would take the beach house. All the property was put into a corporation, overseen by their business adviser, isolating Kathy and Timmy from the property.

Oceanfront property was much sought after, and those seeking it could be a real pain in the butt. Since they had no desire to sell, they preferred not to be bothered. Kathy used the house when she was free from school and had a lady who lived there full-time to take care of the place. Timmy used the beach house when he got a break from school. They saw each other occasionally. Timmy was graduating in June and was seeking a position as an architect in the area. He was looking for a rental, until he got settled.

Chapter Six

TIMMY

As Timmy was completing his senior year of college, he was undecided if he should go into the workforce or go on and get his master's degree. He had interviews with a number of top companies and had received several really good offers. Although the salaries were outstanding, he wasn't sure if he wanted to work for a large company. He had an interview set up for the following day with a local one-man company. He was in no hurry to make a decision, and he was interested to see what a small company had to offer.

The next day, dressed in gray slacks, white shirt, and a blue blazer, he walked into the office of Anderson Construction Corp. The company was located in a new suite of offices in a downtown office building. When Timmy walked in, he was greeted by a young, very good looking receptionist. She asked him his name and told him the boss would see him in a couple of minutes. In just two minutes, the receptionist told him to go on in.

The office was wood paneled, with a large wooden desk, a very nice executive chair, and papers all over the place. The boss, Greg Anderson, was in the middle of the mess. He was wearing blue jeans, a belt with a silver buckle, and a Georgia Tech T-shirt. He motioned Timmy to sit down and said, "Normally it would be correct to apologize for this mess, except this isn't a mess but organized chaos that only an engineer could appreciate." Timmy smiled.

Greg continued, "You're ready to graduate, how many offers have you had? You don't have to answer that. Seeing your college record, I'm sure you've had a lot." After a pause, he asked, "Why would you want to work for me?"

Timmy look straight into Greg's eyes and said, "I'm not sure if I do, but I wanted to compare working for a small company versus a large organization, or if I should go ahead and get a master's."

Greg, with a smile on his face, said, "You know, you don't look old enough to carry water for construction worker."

"As they say, been there, done that. I worked for my father. He owned a construction company. I worked in all phases of the home construction business. My father made sure I started at the bottom and worked up," said Timmy. "Someday I'll grow a beard and look like an adult. Until then, what you see is what you get."

"No offense meant."

"None taken."

"Good. Let's get down to the purpose of this interview: can you be of help to me, and what can I offer you," said Greg. "First, as you know, this is a small operation, and it will probably stay that way, as I want to be totally involved in everything.

"Right now, in the technical portion of the business, we have a structural engineer and an architect—that's me. Anything we can't handle we contract out. We have a management section, a small drafting department, and a crew of senior construction people. Their job is to supervise the contractors who do the actual work. What I need is an assistant to do the nitpicking part of the job. It may be boring, but the person would learn what an architect really does.

"The responsibility would increase with the learning curve. It would give me more time for the management portion of the business. For you, you would learn those small things they don't teach in college. If you decide you want to go with a large company, I would recommend going for a master's degree, otherwise your first year or two will be working as a glorified draftsman. Questions?"

Timmy hesitated and asked, "What are you working on now, and what's coming up?"

"We are finishing up an eight-story office building and will soon start on a one-hundred-twenty-room motel. We have a couple contracts under consideration which will require a complete design of two new buildings. Since your father had a construction business, you know there is a lot involved in starting from scratch and ending up with a completed structure. I love being involved in every detail, and that's what I'm looking for in an assistant. Think about it. You have a great future whichever way you go. Decide what you really want, and choose the road that will lead to your dream. Think about it. I'll send you an offer, but again, think about it before you make a decision. If you have any questions, give me a call. If you like, come out to our construction site and look around and meet the crew. Ms. Good-looking can give you directions to the site."

Greg stood up and extended his hand. Timmy shook it and thanked him for his time. On the way out he asked Ms. Good-looking about directions to the site.

After he left, Greg came out and said to Gladys (Ms. Good-looking), "I like that boy."

Timmy made a trip to the work site and met Jack Love, the mechanical engineer, and some of the construction supervisors. He was impressed with the operation and decided to accept Mr. Anderson's offer. His experience working with his father allowed him to work with the construction crews on their level, and he soon became a "one of us" member of the group. He felt very comfortable in his job and looked forward to going to work every day.

Chapter Seven

THE CRIME

T immy was up early. He showered, dressed in jeans and a T-shirt, and left for work on his bike. They were working at the building site today. Anderson Construction Corp. had an executive suite of offices downtown, but most of their time now was spent at the eight-story building that was almost completed. They had converted the unfinished eighth floor into two sections using plywood panels. The smaller section was for the boss. It was furnished simply with a heavy, old, battered oak desk, an executive chair, a drawing board, a large table for viewing drawings, a couple of filing cabinets, and of course a computer. The other section was for Timmy and Jack, the mechanical engineer. It had two drawing tables, two desks with computers, and assorted chairs and stools. It also had a table for the coffee pot and accessories.

Timmy stopped on the way to pick up some donuts. Although he was half an hour early, the boss was already hard at work. Timmy walked by and said, "Howdy, Boss. Want a donut?"

"Sure, and some coffee if you don't mind," Greg replied.

Timmy went into his section, and as he made the coffee he heard Jack walk in and talk with the boss. Privacy was not a luxury of the offices; footsteps and conversations were heard throughout the floor. Any confidential business was conducted at the office downtown.

The boss had many visitors during the day. First would come the foreman of the crew to discuss the work schedule for the day and any problems that had come up. After that would be a succession of people including contractors, salesmen, and potential customers. Jack and Timmy learned to tune out the conversations, noting when someone came in, but ignoring the conversations.

They were working on the installation for the air-conditioning unit that would be on the roof. One afternoon at about two, they heard footsteps; it sounded like a number of people.

They didn't pay any attention to the talking until it suddenly got loud and angry.

They heard the boss say, "Certainly I know who you are. You're Duke, the union sleaze. I'm not interested in any discussions with you or any union guy. I pay my people their worth, give them good benefits, and treat them fairly. Most have been with me for years and are not interested in a union. Other than that, all my work is contracted out. People problems are their responsibility. If they have unions or not is their problem. I just hire them to do a job."

The next voice, which Timmy and Jack took to be Duke's, said, "Well, mister high and mighty, what if your next building is delayed because the contractors you hired have union problems? Work with me and I can see that there will be no problems, and in the end we'll both make money."

The boss was very mad and yelled, "Take your hooligans and get your ass the hell out of my building. I don't take threats and I don't pay bribes. Security is on its way."

We heard Duke's voice loud and shrill: "No shit talks to me like that. Take him, Snake."

Jack and Timmy knew that the boss had hit the emergency button to alert security that there was a problem on floor eight.

Buttons for emergencies were installed on all floors during construction.

Jack was out of his chair heading for the door to the other room and Timmy was right behind him. Jack had opened the door and taken a couple of steps when someone stepped behind him whacked him hard with an object that Timmy took to be a blackjack. Jack went down and was out cold. Timmy hesitated, saw someone hit the boss on the head and saw him go down. At that instant, Timmy was hit a glancing blow that knocked him down but not out. Two thugs grabbed him and before he could do anything used plastic ties to tie one of his arms to one leg of the desk and his other arm to another leg. They then placed a piece of tape across his mouth.

Lying on his back, Timmy's view was limited. He could see Jack lying on the floor; his hands had been taped so it looked like he was wearing one big mitten. Timmy turned, trying to see the boss. He could hear Duke say, "Let's drop him down that chute, Snake." He saw Duke and another man carrying him, but they were soon out of view. Timmy heard a thump as something or someone went down the chute.

Duke said, "Let's get out of here," and then to the others, "Take care of those two and be sure to send a message."

"Sure thing, Boss," was the reply, in a Russian accent.

Timmy thought he heard the elevator, but he was sure Duke and company had taken the stairs. He then saw the two thugs go to Jack, one standing over him and the other kneeling down and unbuckling Jack's belt. He unzipped Jack's trousers and pulled down his undershorts. The two were grinning at each other and giggling like a couple of teenagers. The one standing removed a switchblade from his pocket and pressed the button; out came a five-inch blade. Looking at his partner, he reached down and grabbed Jack's penis and with one smooth swipe quickly cut it off.

More giggling as he put it into Jack's mouth. The other one quickly put tape across Jack's mouth. Although Timmy had thought Jack was still unconscious, he gagged and his hand went to his mouth in an attempt to remove the tape, but the way his hands were bound it was impossible to grasp the tape and remove it. He gagged and struggled to no avail.

The two thought that was hilarious. They then turned to Timmy. He tried to kick and roll, but one sat on his legs and began to unbuckle his belt and pull down his jeans. He would never forget the look on the one with the knife; it was a look of sheer pleasure. They were both chuckling as he grabbed Timmy's penis and severed it. Timmy didn't know what else happened—he thought he heard the outer door open and gunshots—before he passed out.

As security guards rushed through the door and saw Jack on the floor with blood in a pool around him, they drew their weapons. At the same time, the two hoods drew theirs, but the guards were faster and more accurate. Both of the hoods were killed instantly. Two medics arrived and began to work on Timmy. They reduced the bleeding as much as they could and moved him to a waiting ambulance. The hospital was close by, and in a short time he was in the operating room. They gave him blood and attended to his wound.

As the saying goes, the next thing he knew, he woke up in a hospital bed and saw what he thought was a very attractive nurse. He was right that she was attractive, but wrong about her being a nurse. She was a very talented and experienced plastic surgeon. Her name was Dr. Samantha Webb, and she specialized in putting people back together. Fortunately she was there when Timmy was brought in.

She asked him how he felt, and he muttered something. She then said, "I think you need more rest, but first a couple of people want to ask you some questions. Only five minutes—or if you don't feel up to it, we'll wait until tomorrow. OK, gentlemen, five minutes max or until I say stop."

The two men introduced themselves as detectives. Before they had a chance to ask Timmy anything, he asked them how the boss and Jack were doing. They looked at each other: the boss? Timmy started to black out but managed to say "drop chute." He heard the doctor say, "That's all for now. Maybe tomorrow."

In the waiting room, detective Lieutenant Feinstein and detective Sergeant Mulligan looked at each other with the same question on their minds: the boss? They had only found Jack, Timmy, and the two thugs. Jack had died, as had the two thugs, who were shot and killed in a gun battle with security guards.

They drove back to the construction site, now closed off as a crime scene. There were several uniformed police officers and a company guard standing near the entrance. They greeted the cops and were introduced to the guard, Brian Leigh. They asked Mr. Leigh about the boss and where they could find him.

"Funny," Leigh said, "I haven't seen him since yesterday morning when he came to work."

"He was here yesterday morning. Did you see him leave?" questioned Feinstein.

"No, but he's in and out quite a bit during the day. He's starting another building and goes to that site quite often."

Mulligan chimed in, "We've been calling his house and office, but we haven't been able to get ahold of him. Does 'drop chute' mean anything to you?"

Leigh replied, "Yeah, that big yellow tube running up the side of the building is called the drop chute. There's an opening on each floor so debris can be thrown in. It goes into a large bin at the ground level."

The detectives walked over to the bin; it only took a glance. Feinstein turned to Mulligan. "Call headquarters and have them send the coroner and the lab team to check the bin."

* * *

Timmy awoke early, and the attractive lady was looking down at him. Smiling, she said, "Well, good morning. How do you feel?"

Timmy answered, "Sore and hungry."

"Hungry is good, but I'm afraid the soreness will take some time to go away. I'll see you get something to eat, and if the pain becomes too much, tell the nurse and she'll give you some pain medicine. Other than that, you should be fine considering the ordeal you went through. Later I'll go through what I did and what you'll need to do. After you've eaten, and if you feel up to it, the two detectives want to talk to you. I'll be around if you need me," and with that she walked out.

A nurse, younger but not as attractive, came in and introduced herself. "I'm Mary and I'll be on duty until seven p.m. If you need anything just push the call button. Your breakfast is on the way. Oh, here it is now."

The tray was brought in and put on the bed tray. Mary raised the bed and noticed the pain on Timmy's face.

"Sorry," she said and he nodded. She moved the tray so he could reach it, and asked if he needed help. He assured her he didn't and began to eat. Before she left she told him not to touch his bandages and not to move too much.

As he finished eating, Dr. Sam came in and asked if he was ready to talk with the detectives. She said she would be there and if he showed any sign of stress, she would kick them out.

"Before they talk to you," she said, "I want to tell you what happened. Both Greg and Jack are dead. The two men who attacked you are dead, killed by security and police. That's all that the police know. At least that's all they are reporting. They hope you can help."

"I can," Timmy sobbed. "I know who killed Greg." She quickly went and escorted the detectives in.

Feinstein and Mulligan came in, and without any greeting, Feinstein asked, "Do you know who killed your boss?"

Timmy in a weak and sobbing voice said, "It was a union boss named Duke and a man he called Snake."

"Duke Cavuto and Snake Baer," Mulligan said. "Could you identify them?"

Timmy nodded and then said, "Those two and probably one of the other two. The one with the knife, not the other one."

Feinstein looked at Dr. Sam and indicated he wanted to see her outside. He told Timmy he would see him later and he left followed by Mulligan and Dr. Sam.

In the waiting room, he explained to Dr. Sam that he didn't want the information Timmy gave him to be made public and that he was going to put round-the-clock security on his room.

"Is he in danger?" queried Dr. Sam.

"If Duke Cavuto is involved and he knows that there is a potential witness, yes, he could be in big danger. We'll try to check Duke's whereabouts on that day, before he knows he's a suspect, and if you can, don't make it known that Timmy has regained consciousness."

When Dr. Sam came back into the room she sat down in the chair next to the bed. She relayed what Lt. Feinstein had said, and that the hospital would cooperate completely with the police. She had talked to Timmy earlier about his family. He told her he only had a sister and she was in France going to school. He didn't want to tell her his problem, as she would want to come home and that would interrupt her studies. He would call her after he was out of the hospital and could give her a complete report.

Dr. Sam told him of her knowledge of cases like his. Her husband was an FBI special agent and had considerable experience in protecting witnesses. She explained that although Timmy had witnessed the murder, unless they could get proof that the murderers were at the site, it would be his word against theirs, and the district attorney might not want to go to court unless he had more evidence.

Timmy blurted, "But I saw them do it."

Dr. Sam took his hand and in a soft, quieting voice, said, "I know, dear. Hopefully, the police will be able to break any alibi that they have. Now rest and we'll talk later."

At home later that night while they enjoyed an after dinner drink, a very old cognac that had been a present from a grateful patient, Dr. Sam talked to her husband, David, about Timmy and his problem. They only occasionally discussed each other's professional life, since both had an obligation for secrecy. They did it when one of them had a problem with which they needed help—sometimes just moral support, sometimes help in thinking it through.

They both knew when the other felt uncomfortable about discussing a subject and backed off. Although David made it clear at the beginning that he could do nothing unless the local police asked for assistance, he was happy to discuss what could be done if Cavuto was not indicted or was not found guilty. David was aware that the union boss was vicious and that Timmy would need some kind of protection. Sam told David that Timmy would like to stay at home, but if he couldn't he would go out west somewhere and start a new life. He had money from his parents and could do anything or nothing, without worrying about living expenses. He figured it wouldn't be good to be an architect, but said he could always get a job in construction, maybe build a construction company like his father.

David explained that to start a new life Timmy would have to build an old one, starting with a birth certificate, driver's license, social security card, school records, credit cards, draft card, and credit records. If he had a lot money they would have to set up an account that he could access without it being traced back to him. David said those things could be done but would take time, and a safe house would have to be found for Timmy until then.

Sam walked over, sat on his lap, put her arms around him, and gave him a big kiss.

"Gee, what do I get if I get it done?" asked David.

"I'm sure you'll be pleased," Sam said with a smile.

The next day, David happened to be in the waiting room, waiting for Sam to check on Timmy, when Lt. Feinstein came in. They knew each other and went through the usual greeting and chitchat people in the same profession go through, asking about mutual acquaintances and police business in general, when Feinstein asked, "What's your interest in this case?"

David answered that he had no official interest, but Sam had taken a liking to the kid and asked about what could be done if he had to go into hiding.

Feinstein gave him a look of surprise and said, "Sorry, I didn't make the connection. Dr. Sam is your wife."

Before he finished, Dr. Sam walked out of Timmy's room and David said, "Speak of the devil."

Sam gave him her impression of a scowl and replied, "Why don't I like the sound of that?"

David jumped in before she had a chance to say more. "The lieutenant was saying how lucky I am to have such a beautiful and talented wife."

Feinstein chuckled and said, "Those were my thoughts exactly, but I would never have the nerve to say it. The FBI is so good with smooth talk."

Sam held up her hands and said, "I give up. If you want to talk to Timmy, he's awake, but don't overtire him."

Feinstein started in, stopped, and asked David if he would like to join him.

The three of them walked into the room. Timmy was watching a replay of last night's ball game. As they walked in, he turned off the TV.

Sam placed her hand on his forehead and brushed back his hair. She said, "You know the good looking one, Lieutenant Feinstein. The other one is my husband, David," and she turned around and left the room.

Timmy was smiling and said, "She's something, isn't she?"

David answered, "I think so, sometimes."

Lt. Feinstein brought Timmy up to date on the status of the investigation. They had not been able to break Cavuto's alibi, and the DA wouldn't take any action until he was convinced he had an absolute winning case. He was afraid of Cavuto, who was a big noise in union and local politics. Since it might be some time before they got a break, Feinstein said, they should give thought to Timmy's safety when he leaves the hospital. Timmy had told him that if he couldn't stay in the area then he would like to go out west and start a new life. Lt. Feinstein turned to David and ask if the FBI could assist them in getting papers for Timmy.

"You put in the request, and I'll personally see that it is approved. Anything to keep peace at home," said David. Both Timmy and the lieutenant smiled.

Sam came back into the room and said it was time for the men to leave, and set about making Timmy more comfortable. As David was leaving, he turned to Timmy and quipped, "Young fellow, I'm getting a little jealous, and remember FBI agents have big guns."

"And big mouths. Now, get," interrupted Sam.

Timmy had a big smile on his face and said, "He's something else."

In the waiting room, Feinstein said he would have the request on David's desk the first thing in the morning. "Liking that kid seems contagious." David nodded in agreement.

Lt. Feinstein and Sgt. Mulligan spent the rest of the day finding where Duke had spent his day. They didn't want Duke to know he was a suspect yet, so they told everyone they were checking on the two men killed during the shootout. They made the rounds of the haunts of those types asking questions until they finally came upon Snake. They questioned several others at the establishment before they questioned Snake. They asked all of them where they had been that day and if they knew the two and if they had seen them around the day of the murders. They asked all of them where they had been that day.

When they got to Snake, they asked him the same questions so as not to arouse his suspicion. When they asked him where he was during that day, he answered immediately, almost too quickly, as if he expected to be asked: He had been in a poker game with five other guys at the union hall. When the detectives asked who the men were, Snake got a little defensive and ask why.

The lieutenant answered. "Come on, Snake, you don't hang around with Sunday school teachers. Your cronies may know these guys."

Snake hesitated and gave them four names and, as if it were an afterthought, "Oh yeah, the Duke was there."

"What time was that?"

"We started at noon and played until almost five. We hung around until six shooting the bull."

"All of you?"

"No, Jim and Hank left after the game ended."

The lieutenant hesitated as if he were trying to think of something, and finally said, "You win?"

Snake responded, "Nah, Duke was the big winner. Anything else?"

"No, can't think of anything, thanks."

They talked to a couple of others just to keep up the ruse and left. They got into the lieutenant's car and set off for headquarters.

"Well, we got a start. Now to see if we can break that poker game alibi," murmured the sergeant. "How do we start?"

"First, we'll go back and run checks on those at the poker game and see if there is anything we have that may help," replied the lieutenant.

* * *

David received the request and immediately began the process of developing an old life for Timmy. They found a town in Vermont where records for the two years prior to Timmy's birth had been destroyed in a fire. They would make him a year older, and make the day and month the same as his mother's birthday, hopefully making it easier for him to remember. When the date and place of birth was established, the rest would quickly follow.

David had asked Sam when Timmy would be ready to leave the hospital. She said at a minimum he should stay at least another two weeks, but since she was his attending physician, she could keep him there as long as she liked. They started planning when and how they would get him out of the hospital.

Sam decided that he should stay for at least a month to be sure he was completely well and able to travel. David said that would give him plenty of time to have all the papers ready that Timmy would need. It was decided that only the two of them would be involved in getting Timmy out of the hospital, not even telling Lt. Feinstein. They would tell him after the fact and then he could remove the guard outside Timmy's room. They decided that if Timmy continued to heal and improve they would take him out on the Thursday in a month's time.

After swearing her to secrecy, Sam dropped that bit of information to a nurse known to be a gossip, except she said he would leave on the Saturday.

David had a couple of his agents checking to see if there was any one watching the checkout office or the exit for patients leaving the hospital. They reported that during normal work hours they noticed a couple of people hanging out near the checkout area and also where they could see the exit door. The agents had not ascertained any reason for their being there. They also noted that a different delivery van was parked every night in the parking lot near the hospital exit. They had not approached any of the individuals so as not to raise their suspicions that they were known. The agents would wait until Timmy was leaving before taking any action.

* * *

Timmy was gaining more strength each day and had been walking up and down the hall for several days. He was in good spirits and was looking forward to getting out of the hospital. He had discussed his wishes and his future with Dr. Sam and had concurred with her suggestions and the action they would take.

After dinner on Thursday, Dr. Sam and David came into Timmy's room. David had come in a back way, taken the elevator to the floor above, and walked down to Timmy's floor.

Dr. Sam told the night nurse she had given Timmy a sedative and he should sleep for the night. When she was gone, Timmy got dressed and walked with David to the elevator at the end of the hall.

They took the elevator up two floors and got off. They walked to another elevator at the other end of the hall and took it to the laundry in the basement, from where they slowly walked out to the street.

A few minutes earlier, a local patrolman riding around on a golf cart had stopped and walked up to the van parked in the parking lot. He shined his light inside and tried the door. Not seeing anyone inside, he called the station to have them send a wrecker and tow it away. He talked loudly enough for the two men hidden in the back to hear him. He got back on his cart and drove away to make his rounds of the hospital. As soon as he got out of sight, the van took off.

The patrolman had continued around to the back of the hospital to a parked car with two men sitting in it. He stopped and approached the car and asked the men if he could be of assistance. They said they were waiting for someone who was visiting a sick friend. The patrolman told them that they should drive around to the front since that was the only exit open at this time. They thanked the patrolman, started the car, and drove away. At the same time, Dr. Sam was in her car outside the door of the hospital's laundry room and had the car door open when David and Timmy came out. They got in and she drove away.

The next day, Dr. Sam was at the hospital when the day nurse came on duty. She was a friend of many years and a very trustworthy nurse. Dr. Sam explained that she didn't want anyone to know that Timmy was gone. The nurse nodded and every hour or so would go into the room, spend a few minutes, and leave, speaking to the guard each time she visited. They were able to keep up the charade until Saturday, when David called Lt. Feinstein.

Chapter Eight

PENNY

Penny had just received her degree from a small college in New England when she decided she wanted to go law school in Florida and was accepted for the next term. She found a small apartment in a building within walking distance of the university, which was located in the suburbs of Fort Lauderdale. The apartment building was two stories and had eight apartments. Penny's apartment was on the second floor.

The apartment was small, having a bedroom with bath and a combination living-dining room. There was a small but adequate kitchen. One wall of the bedroom was a closet, more than adequate for her limited wardrobe. She had started to increase her wardrobe with clothing suitable for the warmer weather. The apartment was unfurnished except for the kitchen. She found a suitable bed and chest at a used furniture store. She would buy a new mattress and bedding.

At an antique store she found an inexpensive, large rectangular table that she would use as a dining table at one end and a desk at the other. She also found a bookcase, a filing cabinet, and two chairs for the table. She bought, new, an executive chair and a comfortable lounge chair. She would add other items after she moved in. She moved in with her laptop and her wardrobe. So she began a new phase of her life.

As soon as Penny decided to attend law school, she started taking some first-year courses online. Since it would be almost three months before she started school on campus, she hoped to have much of the first-year requirement completed. Penny was smart, dedicated, and hardworking. She had no problem in applying herself to whatever task she undertook. Her schedule would be to get up before 7 a.m., dress in running togs, have a glass of grapefruit juice, and go for a run around the campus. It would be about a two-mile run every morning. When she got back she would have breakfast and start work on her laptop. Occasionally, she would drive south of Miami toward the Keys and run along the beach. It was a place she had come to love and hoped to possibly obtain a piece of land and build a small beach house there.

She had been referred to a local doctor, Dr. MaryAnne Taylor, and had had several appointments with her. She liked Dr. Taylor, and they became friends. Dr. Taylor, realizing that Penny didn't have many friends in town, invited her to a cocktail party she was having to celebrate the opening of her new office. There would be doctors and their wives, other friends of MaryAnne, as Penny now referred to her, and others, people who were associated with the office, about forty in all. Penny would be among the youngest, being at least ten years younger than MaryAnne. When she received the invitation, the first thing that came to mind was what to wear. It was to be a cocktail party at five in the afternoon. She had never been to a cocktail party, and the only thing she knew is what she had seen on TV. She worried about it all day, even looking up cocktail dresses on the Internet. That didn't help. There were dresses of all shapes, lengths, and colors.

Later that evening she called MaryAnne and asked her. She replied that it wasn't really important, but Penny couldn't go wrong with a simple black dress, and she gave her the name of a dress shop she used downtown. They chatted a little longer and MaryAnne said she would see her at the party.

Penny went to the dress shop the next day and told the lady she was a friend of Dr. Taylor, who had recommended her shop. The lady acknowledged that Dr. Taylor was one of her favorite patrons. Penny explained that she was to attend a cocktail party at the doctor's house and wanted a suitable dress, simple and black. The lady looked at Penny, and said, "Obviously you take a petite size. I have some lovely gowns in that size over here." The first was strapless, which Penny quickly dismissed, and the second had a very short skirt, which she also declined.

Penny said, "I would like one with a skirt that falls below the knees, sleeveless, and maybe a high neck. Simple in design, but it could have a full skirt."

The lady said, "I think I have one that meets those requirements," and she went into the back and came out with one.

The bodice was a satin-like material, sleeveless, with a collar. It had a full net skirt. It was smart but not overwhelming.

She went into the dressing room and tried it on. She loved it and immediately started thinking about which slip she would wear with it. Maybe she would buy a new one; she loved fancy lacy slips.

She went to the lady and told her she would take it, and asked if any adjustments could be made. She felt it could be a little snugger at the waist. The lady got her notepad and a tape measure and started pulling and measuring until she was satisfied. She said she would have it ready in two days. Penny could have a final fitting, and if it was satisfactory she could take it. Penny paid and left feeling in high spirits.

Penny had her final fitting as planned; the fit was perfect. She took the dress home and tried it on with different slips and sighed, saying "Guess I have to buy a new one," which she did that afternoon. The party was still three days away.

Penny arrived right on time. There were quite a few people already there, including Dr. Sam and David. MaryAnne met Penny at the door and showed her around, introducing her to her guests, ending with Dr. Sam and David. Penny spent some time with them, discussing what they had been doing. They made a date for lunch the following week.

Penny got a glass of white wine and went and sat on a comfortable couch in the waiting room. She sat and people-watched, a favorite pastime. David sat down and began talking football, knowing Penny was an avid fan of the local team. As they talked, a young man strolled by and David stopped him and asked who did he think would be the quarterback next week. The young man, named Harry, said he thought the coach would have to go with another quarterback after last week's game. Penny said she thought they should stay with the present one and work on getting him better protection. They had a heated debate and before long a crowd had joined the discussion. When Penny realized David was gone, she looked up and saw him and Dr. Sam looking at her and smiling. She smiled back, realizing what David had done.

She found that most of these people usually gathered as a regular group at a local sports bar when the 'Canes were playing away. When they played at home, some would go to the game. Penny thoroughly enjoyed the group and by the end of the evening had been invited to join them the next Saturday. She became a regular with the group.

Chapter Nine

LAW OFFICE

Penny had maintained her daily schedule and was taking her fourth course on the Internet. At this rate she would have completed all the first-level courses required, except one that she wanted to take on campus. While taking a walk she had stopped in a coffee shop for a break and picked up a local weekly newspaper. While scanning it, she found an ad for a part-time receptionist for a local law firm. When she got home she called, and they asked her to come in the next day for an interview.

She arrived at the time specified and found an empty waiting room. She thought, I guess they do need a receptionist. She heard someone typing on a keyboard in the back. The sound stopped and an older, slightly graying lady came out. She had her hair in a bun and was dressed in a white blouse and a dark skirt. She had a cameo brooch on her blouse. She looked all business until she smiled, and then she looked like a favorite aunt.

She apologized for making Penny wait and asked if she was there for the interview. She said she was.

"Let me say first, the title 'receptionist' is a little misleading. This position is more like a receptionist, a typist, a file clerk, and a gofer. You know what that is?"

Penny nodded her head yes, but she had a quizzical look on her face. The lady explained that it meant running any errands that came up, including going out for meals, laundry, or dry cleaning if needed. She said if Penny felt tasks like that were demeaning, they could terminate the interview.

She explained that the last person she had hired kept complaining that running trivial errands was demeaning and finally left. She said she wanted to be upfront so there were no misunderstandings. Penny told her that was not a problem for her. Penny said she wanted to understand the operations of a law office. She was planning on going to law school in the near future and if she could arrange her schedule she would like to continue working part-time.

The lady asked Penny if she could type, if she was computer literate, and if she could work late if the need arose. She answered yes to all the questions—except that if she started school, classes would take preference. The lady said if Penny wanted to try it, she would hire her with the proviso that if, when school started, she couldn't adjust her schedule to be useful to the office then the agreement would be terminated, no questions asked. Penny agreed and thanked her for her honesty.

The lady told her she could start the next day, but grinned and said, "You can fill out all the forms today on your time." She explained that there were three lawyers in the firm, two male and one female. Each had a specialty, and Penny would learn those. Unless a caller asked for a specific lawyer, any of the three would take the call and refer the caller to the correct lawyer. The receptionist was to answer the phone, but if she was unavailable, the office manager would answer, or, finally, any of the law partners.

The lady said her name was Harriet and her title was 'office manager,' which was as misleading as 'receptionist.' She did the typing, took dictation, did the work of a paralegal, kept the in-house books, and acted as mother hen for the firm. The three lawyers were young and had just formed the firm a few years ago, the reasons for frugality in the office.

The business was growing, but she insisted that they maintain a tight ship. She told Penny that Donald, the senior partner, was her son. Penny could see the pride on her face and understood her concern for the firm, and she took a strong liking to her. Harriet showed Penny where the computer was, gave her a list of forms to fill out, and told her to set up a file for herself and print out two copies of each form. Penny sat down at the computer. Harriet left to continue with her work. She was efficient: from the tasks she assigned, she would know if Penny could follow simple instructions, use a computer, and type. Penny finished her tasks, picked up the hard copies, and gave them to Harriet, who glanced up, nodded, and said, "See you at eight," and returned to her typing.

Penny headed for home, realizing she had a job, even if it was only a couple of hours a day.

The next day, she was up early. She drank her grapefruit juice, put on her jogging clothes, and took off on her morning run. She was back before seven, hot and sweaty. She stripped off her clothes and took a quick shower. She put on her underwear, grabbed a housecoat, and went to prepare breakfast. While doing breakfast she was thinking about what to wear—not that she had much choice. Her wardrobe consisted of mainly skirts, sweaters, and blouses, plus two dresses. She would take her cue from Harriet and wear a skirt and a white tailored blouse. She finished breakfast and went to her closet and removed a dark-gray slim-line skirt and a crisp white blouse. She put on panty hose, a white bra, and a white slip. She finished by putting on the skirt and blouse and ran a comb through her hair and put it in a ponytail. She slipped on a pair of black low-heeled pumps and looked in the full-length mirror. She shrugged her shoulders and figured that was as professional as she could get. She grabbed a sweater and headed for work.

Penny arrived ten minutes early. Harriet was at her desk typing. She barely looked up and said, "If you like, grab a coffee, and when I'm through here, I'll fill you in on our routine," and she returned to her typing.

Penny got a mug of coffee and went to the desk in the reception room. She sat down and turned on the computer. The screen came on showing a logo of the law firm: Dwight, Johnson, and Smyte. That was Donald Dwight, Simon Johnson, and Ellen "Ellie" Smyte.

Harriet came over and explained that Ellen handled criminal law cases for the office, although mostly she was involved in family law including divorce, family abuse, and adoptions. Simon was a financial advisor and handled cases involving wills, trusts, and so on. Donald was the corporate lawyer.

"You'll eventually find out what each really does. Remember, they will talk to anyone and advise what legal service they need, even steer them to another law firm if we can't help them. This attitude has helped us to build a very good reputation," said Harriet, "The office officially opens at nine a.m., which gives us an hour to get ready. The lawyers come in at different times depending on their schedules."

She reached over and hit the return key on the keyboard. Up came a menu for office activities. The first page was that day's schedule from 8 a.m. to 9 p.m. with the lawyers' appointments. It showed Ms. Smyte had no appointments and would be in the office all day. The other two had appointments and would be out of the office all morning, but had several appointments there in the afternoon. Harriet said that meant Ellie would be in sometime before 9 a.m. and the other two would be in sometime after lunch. Ellie was right on time and arrived at 9 a.m. sharp.

Penny liked her right off and was sure she would enjoy working there. The rest of the day, Penny was occupied with some typing, answering the phone, and meeting the other two partners. By 2 p.m. She was ready for a hot bath and a nap. She said goodbye to Harriet—"See you tomorrow"—and headed home.

She had her bath and a short nap, thinking, this is going to be the routine for a while. She dragged out her laptop and began the course she was working on, constitutional law.

The next month, she followed a similar routine. Eventually, Ellie would ask her to do research on some cases she was working on and later on let her sit with her at the defense table during court. Penny took it all in: how the jury reacted to various testimonies and how they were presented, how the judge reacted to the different counselors. She noticed the judge would give an edge to counselors who showed respect. She watched how the two counselors presented their cases.

Sometimes she felt she was in class, and she made the most of the experience. When school started she was able to work only six to eight hours a week. Harriet let her continue because they liked her and she did her job well. They hired another girl who was adequate, not exceptional. Penny did more research for Ellie and handled some of the paperwork. She continued working there until her graduation.

Chapter Ten

PENNY CADET

During her second year, Penny took a course in police procedures and methodology. The course included six weeks at the sheriff's academy during the summer vacation. The students would follow the same physical training as the cadets and take classes dealing with police procedures. Penny was looking forward to participating; she had kept her schedule of physical training and had continued the martial arts classes that the college offered. Her father had taught her to shoot at an early age, and she had become quite proficient with a handgun. She felt she was ready.

There were sixteen students enrolled, ten men and six women. They were housed in barracks at the sheriff's academy and were issued basic training uniforms. The morning would start with physical training, followed by a run over an obstacle course. This would be followed by classes in police procedures including apprehension, arrest, and booking. The afternoon would be martial arts classes and weapons training.

Penny, being the smallest in the class, was at first taken lightly in the martial arts classes, that is until a few of the "big boys" found themselves lying on their backs looking up at her sweet, innocent smiling face. Even after they learned she was not to be treated gently, she held her own.

The martial arts instructor, Sgt. Bell, was impressed with Penny's performance and invited her to help her with a demonstration. After she had explained and demonstrated the technique for the day, Sgt. Bell continued the match with Penny. Neither gained an advantage until Penny hesitated and Sgt. Bell was able to pin her. When Sgt. Bell dismissed the class, she ask Penny to see her after she showered.

"Penny," Sgt. Bell said. "I think I am very good at what I do, and that includes knowing when someone deliberately fails to take advantage of an opponent who makes a mistake. Want to tell me why?"

"Sorry, Sergeant, I didn't know it was so obvious."

Sgt. Bell replied, "Probably not to anyone else."

"Watching you, I noticed that in certain throws you set your feet in a particular position. Let me show you." Penny took the position and continued, "Whenever you get in that position, your follow on is always the same. I took a move to counter that. I didn't follow through, because you are an outstanding instructor and I didn't think giving some jerks in the class an opportunity to have few giggles at your expense was worth it."

"Thank you for that and the lesson. I think I can put it to good use. I have a very dear friend who has been whipping my ass on a regular basis. Now I know why. Won't she be surprised?" said Sgt. Bell.

Since learning how to shoot at a young age, Penny had continued firing on a regular basis. She fired mostly a Beretta 22, although she had a 9 mm Beretta in the house for protection. The cadets fired Glocks since they were used by the sheriff's department. They would practice with 22s, much cheaper to fire. Penny was thus able to use her own weapon to practice. She was an excellent shot and soon earned the nickname "Annie Oakley."

Penny graduated at the top of her class. Those students that completed the course—nine out of sixteen did—were offered the opportunity to join the Sheriff's Auxiliary Corp, a group that assisted the department when additional manpower was needed, mostly for crowd control. They were given identification cards and badges. They had no arrest authority but were given a permit to carry a concealed weapon. They could also volunteer to ride with a senior police officer on an evening patrol. Penny volunteered about once a month. The patrols were mostly uneventful—traffic violations, family squabbles, an occasional convenience store holdup, nothing too dangerous. The officers she rode with saw to that.

On the last Friday of the month, she was assigned to ride with Captain O'Riley. It would be mostly in the university area, just cruising around showing the flag, so to speak. When she got in the car, the captain asked if she had a weapon, knowing they were permitted to carry. He asked what kind.

She answered. "A Beretta 22."

"Think that is heavy enough?"

"It's a weapon I'm comfortable with."

"Guess it really doesn't matter. I've been on the force for twenty-seven years and I've only had to take my weapon out three times," commented the captain. "First it was to use it as a club to subdue a guy high on dope, and the next time it was to impress a young lady."

"Did it work?" Penny asked.

"We've been married thirty-two years. The last time was to apprehend a murderer. I shot him in the leg enabling his capture. Hopefully you'll never have the need to use it, but you might consider carrying the nine millimeter." said the captain.

"I'll consider it," Penny replied.

That evening there were the usual frat house parties that got out of hand. Just the appearance of the police was usually enough to quiet them down.

In the middle of the evening they received a message saying a convicted killer had escaped and was thought to be in the area, and a description followed. Almost immediately a message advised Captain O'Riley the escapee was one he had arrested, and the man had threatened him at the trial. When the captain read the message, he just shrugged. "That happens all the time. We'll keep our eyes open but won't get overly excited by it."

They continued their tour without any excitement. The captain's final stop on his tour was Gallop Park in the university area, a favorite place for students, lovers, and drunks. The captain usually routed out several couples per visit.

The park was about one hundred yards square with crosswalks down the middle dividing the park into four equal squares. They parked at the south end of the north-south walk. The car lights illuminated the entire walkway. As the captain got out of the vehicle, Penny noticed two couples making their way out of the park.

The captain took his flashlight and began his walk around the park. It was easy to follow his progress by watching his flashlight. He stopped a couple of times and Penny could see people leaving. He wasn't interested in arresting anyone, just clearing the park.

Penny watched him cover the park and begin to come down the walk to the car. When he passed the midway point, he stopped and turned. The light from his flashlight showed the face of a man, an angry man. It looked like the man in the bulletin. There was only a riot gun in the cruiser, not good at fifty yards. Penny dug in her knapsack and got her Beretta.

She kept her eye on the captain; he appeared to be kneeling. She opened the door on the driver's side and got out. The window was open and she used the sill as a rest, keeping her eyes on the two men. She reached in and hit the light switches. The world came alive: blue and red lights began flashing, the siren went on, and the headlights lit up the walkway. The escapee looked up, a surprised expression on his face.

She fired three times. Seconds later she saw one man get up. The flashlight waved and she saw the captain standing there. She started to run down the walkway. When she got to the captain, he was standing there looking down at the other man. He was almost as shaken as she was. She thought, "I've just killed for the first time," and she started to shake.

The captain put his arm around her shoulder and they stood there until they were composed, and he said, "What did you use?"

She replied, "My Beretta."

He wanted to say something, but nothing came out. Finally, he just sputtered. "That's a tough way to make a man eat crow." She laughed and he smiled. "Let's go check in."

When they had got to the squad car and turned off the lights, the captain called in, requesting a homicide detective and the coroner. He turned to Penny and said, "I'll have to have your weapon until the investigation is completed. I'm sure there will be no problem."

Penny asked, "Captain, is there any way I can avoid being identified as the shooter? I know it won't be good for me, and I think it could be a problem for the department."

"Are you sure you don't want to be recognized? It might mean a citation and a reward."

"Thanks, but I don't want either, and the press would have a circus."

"You might be right. Let me check with the chief. Go wait over there and avoid everyone."

Someone had called in about the shots and the noise from the squad car. Police cars began to arrive in response to the call. The captain assigned some to control the crowd that began to gather. The coroner and a crime lab truck arrived and started to look after the body. The crime scene was taped off and tasks usually performed at the death of a person begun.

The arrival of the chief caused a rush by the press trying to get information on what had happened. The chief made the usual comment: "No comment at this time. We will have a news conference when we have all the facts."

The chief went to the crime lab truck, together with the captain, the lead detective, and a couple of his aides. The captain gave a rundown of the event including how Penny saved his life and stopped the suspect from continuing his crime spree. He also told the chief about Penny's request to remain anonymous.

After some thought and input from those present, the chief began by saying, "I think Ms. Penny is right. Naming her as the shooter would not benefit anyone, and if she doesn't want the notoriety I think the least we can do is protect her as much as we can. I like the idea of an undercover agent. We can put Ms. Penny on our undercover roster, and we won't have to fabricate a story. Tell her of our decision and see that she gets home without any fanfare. Also set up a meeting where I can meet this young lady. Set a news conference in two hours. By that time, have all pertinent information on my desk and make it known that Ms. Penny's activities are classified 'department secret.' Note: releasing 'department secret' information is grounds for immediate dismissal."

Chapter Eleven

PENNY THREE SHOT

It was a Friday evening and Penny was scheduled to ride with Lt. O'Malley. It was to be a routine patrol through the university campus and adjacent neighborhood. There were reports of noisy frat parties, a couple of family squabbles, one convenience store robbery, and a few traffic violations. The arrival of a police car was enough to quiet down the frat party. The family squabbles took a little time and lots of patience, enough of each to allow both parties to cool off and settle down. There was no violence involved and no arrests made. The police car arrived at the convenience store just as the perp came running out. When confronted by an armed cop, he decided to surrender without resistance. They took him to the station and booked him.

They took a break and had their dinner at a local diner. When they returned to patrol, they received a call that women needed assistance on Redvine Road. They acknowledged and proceeded to the area. They found a woman standing on the curb, who said she had heard a woman scream about ten minutes earlier inside the house behind her, but nothing since.

The lieutenant told Penny to cover the back, and he went in the front door. As soon as he was inside, he yelled, "Police, show yourself." The lieutenant was in the entrance hall. He proceeded to the living room toward the back of the house. He yelled again and proceeded to the back of the house. He heard a commotion and headed in that direction.

As he passed a dining room window, he looked out and saw Penny, on one knee, with her weapon pointed at the back door. He heard someone trying to get out the back. He looked out and saw the back door fly open and the intruder rush out, holding up his pants with one hand and holding a weapon in the other. When he saw Penny he started to raise his weapon. Wrong move. Penny, without hesitation, fired three times. The perp immediately fell to the floor holding his crotch with both hands. The lieutenant thought he heard him yell, "That bitch shot me."

Their backup came through the back gate and Penny motioned them to the perp. She walked toward him, keeping her eyes on him and her weapon pointed at him. She stepped over him and kicked away his gun and then went into the house, where she heard someone crying and screaming.

The emergency medical technicians arrived and attended to the perp. One of the squad, a woman, immediately went into the house when she heard the crying coming from within. The screaming had stopped, but the crying continued. The assailant was attended to and eventually removed on a gurney. Penny and the EMT came out with the victim between them. They took her to a police car to transport her to the hospital. The lieutenant and Penny got into his car and went first to the hospital to check on the perp and the victim.

They were met by a cop with a smile on his face. "Whoever took him down should get a medal. That's one that will never rape another woman."

The lieutenant responded, "I'll tell the undercover agent."

The cop looked at him. "Copperhead, huh?"

The lieutenant replied. "Copperhead?"

"Yeah, that's the name they gave to the undercover cop who saved the captain. Redheaded and deadly."

The lieutenant thought. "Copperhead, not a bad nickname for Penny."

They checked on the victim. It seems they had arrived in time to prevent a rape. Although she had been beaten up a bit, those wounds would heal.

The perp was not so lucky. All three shots found their mark. They had to remove both testicles and two-thirds of his penis; poetic justice, some might say. Lt. O'Malley and Penny drove to the station and made their report. Penny once again turned her weapon in until the investigation was complete. Mark another up for the undercover agent.

They returned to the station and the lieutenant completed his report. It stated in part: "The suspect, attempting to flee the building, was met outside the back door by an undercover officer. The suspect started to raise his weapon to a position to fire at the officer. The officer fired first, three times, all shots hitting the suspect. The suspect was apprehended and taken to a local hospital. The victim was escorted to the hospital for observation and treatment as necessary."

The lieutenant handed in his report and they headed to the "Lockup," the local cop hangout. The place was full, and drinks were flowing freely. The one word heard above the din was "Copperhead." It was definitely the topic of discussion.

When they walked in, all eyes turned to the door and most looked at Penny. They returned to what they had been doing. One officer stood up, raised his glass, and toasted, "To Copperhead, wherever he may be." There was a slight emphasis on the "he." All drank and returned to their conversations.

Though they all assumed they knew who "Copperhead" was, they would protect that officer's identity. Bits of the conversation would be heard during lulls in the overall noise: three shots in the crotch you could cover with a silver dollar; made him a eunuch; served the bastard right ... then the din took over. When the lieutenant and Penny were leaving, the entire crowd stood up and clapped.

"That was quite a tribute," the lieutenant said. "That's a tough crowd."

Chapter Twelve

COPPERHEAD STRIKES AGAIN

All senior officers were expected to make an evening patrol at least once a month, station policy. Normally, they would take a new patrolman, but Captain Jack decided to have Penny ride with him. It was to be her last tour as she was graduating and would start working at the district attorney's office the next week. He told Penny he had picked what he thought would be an interesting but uneventful hazard-free assignment, as backup, way back, of a drug bust by a SWAT team. They were listed as observers.

They had received information of a meth lab set up in an old factory in the south side. At the appointed hour, the captain and Penny had stationed themselves in position at the very back of the building. They could follow the raid on their headsets. They heard the order to enter the building and the ensuing noise as the door was knocked in. They heard shouts and orders being given, but no shots. All became quiet; mission seemed accomplished.

Penny and the captain at the same time heard noises on the roof. They saw two men creeping along, and both were armed. The captain was positioned near the building and was not able to get a good view of the perps. He moved a little to get a better look, making enough noise to alert the men above. The man closest to the edge was looking directly down on the captain and was taking aim when Penny fired three times. The perp fell, almost falling on the captain, who by that time had moved into a position where he had the other man in his sights. The other man decided not to challenge the 9mm pointed at him and he surrendered.

By the time the SWAT team arrived, the captain had the second man in cuffs. The two men were the head of the local operations and had been able to sneak out as the team broke in.

When the SWAT team leader saw that one of the men had been taken he said, "Great, now we may find the source. These guys are just flunkies."

"Good job for a captain," he said with a smile on his face. "That Glock did a great job."

The captain said, "Look again, the one on the ground was taken with a Beretta 22. The Glock did scare the other one into giving up."

The SWAT team leader looked at the captain and quietly mouthed, "Copperhead?"

The captain only smiled and nodded. The captain and Penny went to headquarters to fill out a report. Once again she turned in her weapon pending an investigation.

As she left, she couldn't resist, "Thanks, Captain, for another uneventful evening." The captain could only smile.

Chapter Thirteen

PENNY THE GRAD

Upon graduating from law school, Penny applied for and was accepted by the district attorney's office. She was assigned to Maxine (Max) Witte's section, specializing in criminal prosecution. Max took her under her wing and let Penny work with her on many cases. As she gained experience, Max let her try minor cases on her own. Penny was a fast study and was soon a full participant in Maxine's section.

Max was in court prosecuting a man accused of breaking and entering. Penny was sitting at the prosecutor's table acting as her assistant. A neighbor was on the witness stand. Max asked him if he had seen a man hanging around the property the afternoon before the break-in, and the witness said yes, he had.

When Max asked if he could identify the man, the witness said yes, and pointed at the accused. The accused, seated at the defense's table, started to get to his feet and yelled, "That's a lie, you!" The deputy behind him put his hands on the defendant's shoulder to restrain him. He shoved his elbow hard into the deputy's stomach and jumped over the table and headed toward the witness stand. Penny, without hesitation, jumped in front of the man. He was moving fast and was off balance. She threw a block and let his momentum carry him over her and onto the floor.

By then several deputies had caught up with the guy and quickly handcuffed him.

The judge rapped the court to attention. "Please remove that gentleman from the courtroom. This court will take a thirty-minute recess."

As the judge walked past, she whispered, "Nice job, Ms. Penny." Max also gave her a thanks.

One of the deputies was heard to remark, "She's almost as good as Copperhead."

Chapter Fourteen

PARIS WITH SAM

D
r. Sam had been invited to chair a discussion on reconstructive surgery at a medical conference in Paris. It was an honor—and a week in Paris. Dr. Sam and Dr. MaryAnne had decided to attend the conference, saying, "It's tough, but someone has to do it." David, Dr. Sam's husband, was on assignment in San Diego. They asked Penny if she would like to join them and make it a girls' week out. They said the conference was only during the day and the shops would be open in the evening. Also there was to be a formal cocktail party on the last day, which gave them an excuse to buy a new dress. Since she was not too busy and she had vacation time that they kept asking her to use, Penny eagerly agreed. A week with those two promised to be most enjoyable.

They met at MaryAnne's house to discuss and plan the trip. When Penny asked about the weather and what to take, and they laughed and said they were taking empty suitcases and would fill them there, she halfway believed them. More seriously, they said the temperature would be mild during the day and a little cool at night, so she should take a couple of sweaters and a light wrap.

Dr. Sam had to attend to some business in New York, so MaryAnne and Penny would meet her there and fly together to Paris. As they could get good deals on airline tickets through the conference, they decided to go first class. They already had booked a two-room suite at the hotel where the conference was to be held, and Penny could share it. MaryAnne had spent a year in Paris during her undergraduate days, and several friends had invited her and her guests to dinner. It would appear to be a full week. They looked at the conference schedule and decided which sessions they wanted to attend. They made a list:

Monday:
Arrive
4 p.m. – Welcoming cocktail party
7 p.m. – Dinner with friends

Tuesday:
Morning free (dress getting)
1 p.m. – Dr. Sam's Session
Evening free

Wednesday:
8 a.m. – 5 p.m. – Sessions
Evening free

Thursday:
8 a.m. – 12 p.m. – Sessions
Afternoon free (shopping)

Friday:
8 a.m. – 11:30 a.m. – Sessions
Afternoon: Beauty Spa
6:30 p.m. – Farewell Dinner

Saturday:
Ready for flight home

Penny had been to Paris some time ago for a few days, enough to be excited for a chance to spend a week exploring the city. She knew that Paris was an easy city to get around: just get on the Metro and it would take you to a new unique neighborhood at every stop. It was a wonderful city to just walk and people watch. The three friends all went home enthused and looking forward to their trip in three weeks. Penny knew she could get all her loose ends at work cleared up by then and could take the trip worry free. Her first real vacation in six years. One good thing: her passport was still valid. Plus, she didn't have to make any of the arrangements, just pick up her bag and follow.

Chapter Fifteen

PARIS

O n Sunday, three weeks later, Penny picked up her bag and laptop and took a taxi to the airport. She and MaryAnne flew to New York, where they met Sam in the first class lounge. Being doctors, they knew drinking alcohol on a long flight was not a good thing, but they ordered three martinis. Penny was not a drinker of the hard stuff, mainly sticking with wine or beer, but the occasion seem to call for it, not that she needed a drink to feel high. The three of them were in high spirits just thinking of the week ahead. After the martinis, they were absolutely giddy. It must have been a spectacle to see three well-dressed women giggling like teenagers.

Penny had not flown a lot—mostly trips associated with work. There, you flew economy only because there was no lower class. This was her first time flying first class, and she intended to enjoy it. The airport lounge was nice, with comfortable chairs and couches and areas to use computers, and it was reasonably quiet. There was also a bar with snacks, goodies, and of course, drinks. Fortunately, they had only a short time before they boarded and were not tempted to have another round. A good thing, for as soon as they took their seats in first class they were offered a glass of champagne. They accepted the offer and clicked their glasses together in a toast for a great week, downed it, and giggled some more.

The seats were large and comfortable and had more buttons than a hospital bed. You could tilt them back until they were almost horizontal and set them in any position in between. They started to play with the buttons, and in their condition everything seemed funny. There were more giggles until the stewardess gave them a dirty look, and then they controlled themselves and settled down.

About one hour into the flight, the stewardess came around with a menu for dinner. There was a choice of three entrees, salad, soup and dessert, and of course, wine. Penny had baked haddock, salad with blue cheese, mixed veggies, and cherry cheese cake. She chose a chardonnay to go with the fish. She could get used to first class. They chatted and ate and giggled and talked all through dinner.

Finally, after turning down an after dinner drink, they put on their provided night socks, reclined their seats, covered themselves with blankets, and tried to sleep. At first Penny's mind was active as she thought about all sorts of things, but finally she fell asleep. It didn't seem long before she heard the stewardess delivering breakfast. Dr. Sam was awake and said it meant they were only about an hour or so from Paris. As soon as she finished breakfast and had a second cup of coffee, Penny went to the lavatory, washed, brushed her hair, and applied some makeup. She was ready for Paris. She returned to her seat just in time to hear the pilot say they were starting their descent into Charles de Gaulle airport.

MONDAY

They passed quickly through passport control and went to pick up their luggage. Sam's and MaryAnne's bags appeared early, and Penny had begun to worry that hers was lost, when it finally came out. They put all the bags on a cart and headed through customs. As they exited the secure area, there was a crowd of people waiting. The conference had arranged limousine service, and the driver was there holding a sign with their names. He took their luggage and directed them to the limo. They headed to the Hotel Lutetia in the Saint-Germain area. He took a route that took them around the Arc de Triomphe and down the Champs Elysees. Penny gawked at the streets and the people of Paris. She loved it.

When they arrived at the hotel, their bags were taken to the reception desk and they checked in. Their suite was on the fifth floor and they could see the Eiffel tower. There was to be a welcoming get-together at 4 p.m. It was mandatory for Sam and MaryAnne to attend, so they would have to be back at the hotel no later than 3 p.m. to get ready. They decided to explore the local neighborhood until then.

The hotel was in an old section of town and they started walking, stopping to window shop. There were shops of all kinds: dress shops, shoe stores, bookstores, antique stores, lingerie shops, and many bistros and restaurants. They couldn't pass the lingerie shop without going in. Once inside, they had to buy something. Without enough time to really look at all the wonderful lines of goods, they proceeded to the panties section. Not totally acclimated to the time change, they were still in a state of mental intoxication.

Dr. Sam, who was without any inhibitions whatsoever, picked up a thong that had less material than one of her hankies, held it up, and asked, "You think this would excite David?"

Penny responded that she doubted if Sam could get him to wear it. That caused them all to burst into laughter, which only increased in intensity as they searched for the most ridiculous panties they could find, and there were many that fell into that category.

They were getting a lot of attention and were only able to stop laughing when a clerk came over and ask if she could be of assistance. Feeling embarrassed and a little guilty for their actions, they each bought three pairs of underwear. Dr. Sam bought two pairs that Penny was sure she would wear only once just to see the expression on her husband's face. Not having anyone she wanted to shock, Penny bought a pair each of white, red, and black panties, plain and conservative. MaryAnne purchased usable but less conservative ones.

Penny thought she would like to do a study to determine if you could guess what type of panties a woman wore and what it would tell you about her personality. She told her friends about her proposed study. For the rest of their walk, they made remarks about different women: those that looked seductive they called "black-lace ladies"; others were "thong girls," "bloomers ladies," or "none ladies" (this of course brought another fit of laughter), and when a plainly dressed business woman came along, Dr. Sam quipped "white cotton." Penny didn't laugh as much as the others, as this hit home. It was a fun walk.

When they returned to the hotel, they went to their rooms so Penny's companions could get ready for their get-together and for dinner later with one of MaryAnne's friends.

As they rushed to get ready, Penny unpacked her computer and connected to the Internet. Twenty-six messages. Twenty-three were junk and she deleted those. There was one from Max wishing her a happy vacation and saying she may have something interesting for her when she got back. Penny sent her a message thanking her for the thought and describing their trip and their activities so far. She deliberately skipped asking what Max might have for her when she got home. She was happy to wait until she got back. As Penny typed, Dr. Sam gave the friends a fashion show of her new undies, amid whistles and laughter. Penny had to retype a lot of her message. She answered the other two e-mails and started to think about getting ready herself.

Her selection of fancy wear was limited to a couple of choices: a blue dress, or a long black skirt with a sheer black blouse. She laid them out on the bed and decided on the skirt and blouse. MaryAnne and Sam were ready and said they would call her from the lobby when they were finished. They assured her it would be no more than an hour.

Penny took a shower, washed and dried her hair, and put on a pair of her new undies, the black ones. She found a black bra and a black slip. As with all her slips, it had a lot of lace. The first time she saw her mother walking around in a very pretty lacy slip, she was hooked. She loved the look and felt they oozed femininity. She brushed her hair, applied what little makeup she used, and redid her lipstick. She finished by putting on her skirt and blouse and a pair of black sheer hose.

Penny really hated high heels and only wore them when the occasion demanded. This was one of those occasions.

When she finished, she looked in the mirror and was satisfied. She got out a small black bag and moved items from her other bag into it. She made sure she had a hanky and tissues. She still had fifteen minutes and decided to go to the lobby and people watch until the girls arrived. They came out of the conference room and it was obvious that the get-together was more than just chatting. Both of their faces were flushed and they were giggling. They look at her and said together, "We only had one, maybe two glasses of champagne." MaryAnne burped.

MaryAnne's friend Marie arrived and took them to her apartment, which was also on the left bank and not far from the Sorbonne. Already at the apartment were Marie's husband, Henri, another couple, Henri and Pauli, and a young woman about Penny's age named Susan. For some reason they started to call her Suzy, which they later learned she hated, but she showed tolerance of her fellow Americans, at least for the evening.

The Henris were professors at the Sorbonne. Marie had an art salon near the school, and Pauli had a small bookstore next door. Suzy was an artist and was spending three months in Paris. She had another month before returning to the US. She was clean and neat, but her selection of clothing said, "I wear what I'm comfortable with, and I'm a free spirit." She was smart, articulate, and funny. Suzy and Penny hit it off from the first. It was a lively dinner with good conversation covering everything from pop music, art, and theater to politics, medicine, and the law.

The meal was everything that Penny thought a French meal would be. It covered everything from soup to cognac, and the wine glasses were never allowed to be empty. So it was a very happy group by the time they had espresso. Since the doctors had an early schedule, they took their leave earlier than they would have liked. Before they left, Suzy asked if she might show Penny around the next day, and when she assured Penny it would not interfere with any of her plans, she said she would be most pleased. With that, Marie took them back to their hotel. It had been a wonderful day.

TUESDAY

The friends were up and dressed early, eager to go dress shopping. Suzy arrived just as they finished dressing. They told her their plans and she suggested having breakfast at a small bistro down the street on the way to the dress shops. Sam and MaryAnne had seen a shop with some dresses in the window that they liked, and they wanted to start there. Penny hadn't seen anything that appealed to her, and she thought her petite size might be problem. Suzy suggested a shop where she could probably find something.

It was owned and operated by Monsieur Philippe, who designed, fitted, and altered the dresses right there in the shop. Penny wondered how expensive they would be, but then thought, expense be damned (within reason, of course). Sam and MaryAnne headed for their shop, and Suzy and Penny headed for Monsieur Philippe's.

The shop was small, and when they entered, Penny noticed there were only about eight mannequins in the round room, fitted with some very attractive dresses. Monsieur Philippe's English was as limited as her French, so Suzy stayed with her to interpret. Penny explained what function she was attending and basically what she wanted.

Philippe looked at her and said, "Petite." He went into a back room and came out with three dresses. The first was strapless, and she shook her head, no, followed by one with puffy sleeves, which she also declined. The third she liked very much: it was sleeveless with a high neck and a triangular cutout low enough to show what little cleavage she had. She told Suzy she would like to try it on, and she relayed this to Philippe. He showed Penny to the fitting room and Suzy told her to undress.

When he brought the dress back and saw her white slip, he made a noise and Suzy told her to remove her slip. Just as she finished taking off her slip, Philippe walked in and handed her a black slip. She was surprised, and she saw Suzy trying not to laugh. Suzy said, "Relax, that's the easy part." Penny gave her a quizzical look.

Philippe reappeared and helped her put on the dress. She took a look in the mirror and thought it looked great.

Philippe stood in front of her with his left hand holding his right elbow and the fingers of his right hand extended, stroking his chin. He was making small noises and nodding his head, but with no expression on his face. Penny didn't think she would want to play poker with him or have him as a member of a jury. He walked around to her back. She was looking at Suzy, who wasn't smiling. Penny was surprised, but then she saw that Suzy's stomach was shaking. Before Penny completed that thought, she felt Philippe's hands on her waist and flowing up as he felt the drape of the material. When his hands got to her shoulders, they moved down under her arms and down her sides to her waist. She then felt him forming the dress around her bottom. He stopped, made some chalk marks on the dress, and made some notes on a pad he had attached to his left arm. He move around to face her, still with the stone face.

Once again he took his stance with his fingers rubbing his chin. He looked her up and down, but she was sure he only saw the flow of material. He leaned his head to the left and to the right and then put his hands at her waist. She looked for Suzy, but she had left the room, maybe for a potty break.

While Penny was thinking of Suzy, Philippe ran his hands down over her thighs, made a couple of chalk marks, and wrote on his pad. Suzy came back in and Penny noticed she was wiping tears out of her eye, and they were not tears of sadness. Then Philippe put his hands at her waist with his thumbs meeting at her navel.

He moved them left and right and watched how the material moved. He then moved his hands slowly up, not touching the material but occasionally stopping and making a mark and a note.

He finally reached her breasts and his hands encircled the bottom of them. Penny looked at Suzy again and could have sworn that in a couple more minutes there would be parts of Suzy all over the wall; she looked like she was going to burst. She walked out again. Philippe pushed Penny's breasts up, and at the same time his hands squeezed them together. She thought she saw an expression on his face. She looked down and actually saw some cleavage. He moved his hands, changing the separation and uplift. Finally he removed his hands and made some more notes and said "Bon" and left.

Suzy had again returned and through restrained laughter said, "So, how did it feel to be ravaged by a zombie?"

Before Penny had time to think of an appropriate answer, Philippe returned and began unbuttoning her dress and helping her remove it.

He took the dress and left, and Suzy quickly followed him. Penny took off the black slip and put on her own clothes. She gave the slip to Philippe and looked at Suzy, who told her Philippe had said the dress would be ready on Thursday at 3 p.m. He had also recommended she go to a bra consultant down the street and get fitted for a bra.

When she saw the look on Penny's face, Suzy hastily added, "Madam Duveau is the bra mistress."

Penny stopped to look at a display of panty hose and was going through the various shades when Philippe came by, picked up a pair, and handed them to her. "Tis right," he said.

After she paid, they left the store and went to see how Sam and MaryAnne were doing. They had both made a selection and were being fitted. Penny and Suzy told them where they were going and agreed that whoever finished first would find the others.

Madam Duveau's shop was a simple, small establishment having a sales room and a couple of back rooms, one for fitting and one for sewing. When they walked in, Madame Duveau came in from the sewing room. Suzy explained they had come from Monsieur Philippe and gave her the note he had written. She read it and said her English was sufficient to do the fitting, and if Suzy cared to wait in the sales room, there were plenty of fashion magazines. If she liked, there was coffee or tea.

Madame Duveau indicated for Penny to follow her into the fitting room and requested that she remove all her clothes above the waist. Penny removed her blouse and lowered her slip to her waist. She removed her bra and stood there naked from the waist up. The woman then made the usual measurements for a bra: chest under the breasts, chest above the breasts, and the fullest part of the breasts. She made additional measurements from the nipple to the shoulder and from nipple to nipple. She also measured the circumference of each breast. After she had finished and recorded Penny's measurements, she said, "One moment, s'il vous plait."

She returned with a weird-looking bra that had adjustable straps and multiple ribbons attached to each cup. She helped Penny put it on and adjusted the straps. When she was satisfied, she started to adjust the ribbons on the cups, pulling and tugging until she had the shape she thought was right for Penny. She explained that the sizing bra, as she called it, was her own design. When she had recorded all the measurements of the different ribbons, she helped remove the bra and told Penny she could get dressed.

She dressed and went to the sales room. Suzy was talking to Madame Duveau and told Penny they could come back at 1 p.m. on Thursday—and would she like more than one? Thinking about it, Penny said she would like one black and two whites.

They left and met Sam and MaryAnne coming down the street. They stopped at a cafe to have lunch and discuss their experiences. Sam and MaryAnne told the others about their dresses. Penny told them about her dress and about getting fitted for a bra. She didn't tell them about Philippe fitting her dress. Suzy didn't say anything, just smiled.

Sam and MaryAnne had to get back for the afternoon session.

WEDNESDAY

The doctors had early lectures and left before Penny was up. They had arranged to have lunch together at a small bistro just down the street at noon.

Suzy was supposed to be at the hotel at 9 a.m. for breakfast, but before Penny was dressed Suzy called to say she had arrived. Penny told her to come up as she would be a couple of minutes. Suzy was wearing a short skirt, tights, a white sweater, and black boots. She had on a long denim coat. Penny was still in her slip. As she put on her skirt and sweater, Suzy asked if she would like to go to the Orsay, an art museum that was across from Notre Dame Cathedral, which they could visit afterward if they had time. Penny was not a great art fan, but when she saw the pleasure on Suzy's face when she talked about it, she readily agreed. Suzy said it was within walking distance and they could stop on the way for breakfast.

They stopped at a small restaurant that had tables outside, but it was a little cool so they sat inside. While having French coffee, croissants, and jam, Suzy told Penny about the Orsay museum and some of the other sights she might like to see. Penny told her how much her offer meant, but said she didn't want to take up all her time. Suzy said she used her time as she wanted, and this week she wanted be a tour guide.

The Orsay had impressionist paintings from the late nineteenth and early twentieth centuries. With Suzy pointing out and explaining different techniques and approaches of the painter, Penny had greater appreciation for the paintings but was still not a great art lover. She did prefer these to the old masters in the Louvre. They finished there and had enough time for a short visit to Notre Dame. Penny lit a candle for her parents and said a short prayer.

MaryAnne had made reservations for lunch at a very famous restaurant that translated to "The Frog and Pickle." Penny thought the French version must sound more appetizing. MaryAnne said she was on the Internet three weeks before they left and this was the only opening available during their time in Paris. She wanted them to have the experience of a Michelin rated restaurant.

Penny and Suzy met MaryAnne and Sam at noon. Their reservation was for 12:30 p.m. There was a long line waiting to get in. Penny thought, thank goodness MaryAnne had the foresight to make reservations and they were able to go right in.

The building was very old and the interior decor was in the style of the eighteenth century. When they were seated they ordered martinis all round. They took the time to take in the ambiance, a word that Penny always thought a little pretentious, but here it seemed appropriate.

Suzy talked her into splitting an appetizer of escargots. Suzy had what Penny would have called a chicken salad, but it had a fancy name and it was definitely different from Penny's. It came with a delicious crème sauce surrounded by an artistic display of raw vegetables. They each had a divine chocolate dessert and an espresso. The escargots were an experience, and the meal was most memorable. Penny thanked MaryAnne for arranging it. They declined an after dinner drink as the doctors had to return for the afternoon session.

Just as they were getting ready to leave, the woman behind MaryAnne began to choke. MaryAnne immediately turned around, evaluated the situation, and put her arms around the lady and performed the Heimlich maneuver. The lady coughed and expelled something from her mouth. She took a couple of deep breaths and seemed to be all right. MaryAnne asked her how she felt, and when she indicated OK with a nod, MaryAnne turned to leave.

They were all starting toward the door when the maître d' went running to talk to the lady. Before they reached the door, the maître d' caught up with them and grabbed MaryAnne's arm. As they engaged in a conversation, his hands were rapidly moving and every other word seemed to be "merci." Suzy explained he was thanking MaryAnne and wanted to express his appreciation in some tangible way. MaryAnne whispered in his ear so no one could hear her. The maître d's face lit up and he had big smile on his face and was nodding his head. After a couple more "merci's" they were able to leave.

When they got outside they asked MaryAnne what she had said to the maître d'. She answered that she had told him to forget it, that any red-blooded American superwoman would have done the same. She refused to discuss it further. The rest of them had the same thought: "MaryAnne is up to something."

The doctors had a full schedule for the afternoon until around 5 p.m. Suzy suggested she and Penny go for a walk down the Champs Elysees. They took the Metro and ended by the Arc de Triomphe. The weather was nice, the sun was shining brightly, and there were few clouds. There were many people walking and sitting at tables along the street.

They strolled, stopping to window shop and sometimes going in and looking. Penny told Suzy she would like to get some skirts and some slips, that she never had too many slips. Suzy said there was a shop a little farther down that had a nice selection. After a short stroll, they stopped at a sidewalk cafe and had a coffee and watched the people walk by. Suzy talked about her time in France. She had spent time in a small seaside village where there were no tourists. She had been there a couple of times, staying a week or so. She painted and relaxed, walking along the rugged shore. She said she might go back once more before she returned home.

Penny told Suzy about her oceanfront hideaway in Florida and said she would very much like for her to visit. She told her about the beaches and the beautiful sunrises and sunsets full of pinks and blues. She almost made herself homesick.

They continued on to the lingerie shop. Suzy had been right, it had a beautiful selection. Suzy asked Penny if she always wore dresses or skirts. She replied, always when she was working and in the city. When she was at the bungalow at the beach, she wore shorts or overalls. She finally settled on three slips, one black full slip and two white half-slips, similar in style and all with lots of lace. Suzy said they were lovely, but didn't seem too enthused. Penny knew people thought she went a little overboard on slips, but it was her obsession and she just loved the feel of smooth silk on her body.

She finished her shopping and they took the Metro back to the hotel. Soon the doctors got back from their last lecture. They came in, threw off their shoes, and flopped on the beds. Penny told them about her and Suzy's walk and asked if they could guess what she had bought. Without even raising their heads, both said "slips." Penny thought, next time I'll buy condoms.

Sam asked if they would like to go down for a cocktail and a quick dinner. They had another early session. They got to the bar and took a table, and before they got their drinks, a group of male doctors joined them —so much for a quick dinner. Penny was embarrassed and pleased at the attention she received. When she was with Sam and MaryAnne, even though she was a grown woman and a successful lawyer, she still felt like a little girl. They seem so self-assured and so at ease with people, both men and women. Being with those two in mixed company might help her gain the confidence she needed in a social setting.

FRIDAY

It was the night of the farewell party. They all met at noon, after the doctors' last seminar. They had appointments to get the works: manicures, pedicures, facials, massages, and their hair washed and set. This was all new to Penny; the only thing she had had was an occasional manicure, and she was a little awed when she walked into the new and very modern salon. First, they spent a short time in a sauna, and this was followed by a massage. Penny could only say that it was luxurious, lying there and having a masseuse pour warm fragrant oil on her back, and sometimes gently and sometimes vigorously massaging her whole body. She became so relaxed that she almost fell asleep.

Done with the massage, she took a shower and went back to the dressing room, where she put on her panties and bra and a lovely pink spa gown. Next was the manicure and pedicure.

They were all talking sitting in a row, each with a lady working on her hands and another lady working on her toes. It was as noisy as dinner time in a chicken pen, with giggles in both English and French (yes, there is a difference, Penny thought). Suzy kept the French ladies in stitches as she gave them her translation of what the friends were saying. Penny knew enough French to know Suzy's translation was anything but literal. Having her hair washed and dried was so pampering that Penny decided she would indulge in the future.

Next was the facial, which she enjoyed but decided it was something she could do herself. The stylist brushed her hair and showed her pictures of various hairstyles, but she decided that she was satisfied with her plain style. She had an almost baby face and was afraid a fancy hairdo would make her look like a little girl with a fancy grown-up hairdo. She decided that if she could not be sophisticated, she would be satisfied with cute. She grimaced and giggled to herself.

Since the others were still having their hair done, the lady plucked Penny's eyebrows. Ouch! She also darkened Penny's eyebrows a little and put mascara on her eyelashes. Once she started, she kept going, putting on eye shadow and some makeup. When Penny was handed a mirror, she saw a stranger. She wasn't sure if she liked the image or not. She kept looking in the mirror and finally decided she would wait and ask the others' opinions.

When they were all finished, they dressed and went back to the hotel and Suzy went home to get ready.

With two bathrooms, one had to wait for one of the other two to finish. Before anyone started, Penny asked them about her makeup. They both came over and looked very seriously at her, saying, turn your head left, now right, now tilt it up a little, now down. She complied with all their directions and awaited a decision.

Sam asked, "Well, what do think, MaryAnne?"

Very quietly, MaryAnne said, "Maybe if we removed her left ear for a little balance."

"Nah," Sam said. "I'd probably have to put it back, and I didn't bring my sewing kit."

Penny was listening so intently that it took a moment to realize what they had just said. She saw the serious looks turn to grins and finally into full laughter. If she had been closer, she might have slugged them.

Before Penny could react, MaryAnne threw her arms around her and said, "Honey, your makeup is perfect. You look lovely. Maybe a little darker lipstick."

Sam was trying to stop laughing and could only nod.

Penny looked at them as if to say "I can't believe you two kooks." She finally grinned and went into the bathroom. Looking into the mirror, she decided they were right and she washed the lipstick off. She would use her regular shade.

She left the bathroom so MaryAnne could use it. The bedroom was empty as both of the others were in the bathrooms. She stripped and put on a pair of nylon no-line black panties, followed by her new fitted bra. She was amazed at the difference it made. It was more comfortable and did add to her shape. She was surprised that it mattered to her. She put on the sheer black panty hose that Philippe had thrown at her. This was followed by a slip that had a bodice of plain black silk and a skirt of black lace.

Sam and MaryAnne both commented on the loveliness of the slip. They had caught up and were standing around in their slips when someone verbalized what they were all thinking: "I wonder what Suzy will wear?"

During their four days with Suzy, she had worn a variety of clothing from peasant to bizarre. The clothes were clean and neat and somehow seemed appropriate on her. As the others thought about it, they had another fit of giggles. They finished dressing, helping each other get their dresses on, zipping them up and seeing that everything was in place and nothing showed that wasn't supposed to show. When satisfied, they put on their shoes, grabbed their purses, and headed down to pick up the fourth musketeer.

They reached the lobby just as Suzy walked in. If she had looked then, she would have seen three ladies with their mouths hanging open. She was stunning in a black formfitting dress with one bare shoulder. She walked over. "Well, aren't we the four merry widows?" she said, looking at the four black dresses.

"I'm not sure about widows, I am about merry," was Penny's reply.

As Penny looked at Suzy's dress, Suzy smiled and said, "Yes, it was designed and fitted by Monsieur Philippe." Penny grinned, thinking about Philippe running his hands all over that shapely body to be sure the material formed perfectly to it. He had done a fantastic job. She wondered if he ever had any emotion during his work. She would have to ask Suzy how she felt.

Sam said, "Shall we go?" and led the way into the ballroom and directly to a large table being used as a bar. They each took a glass of champagne, and before they had a chance to take a sip, they were joined by four doctors looking elegant in their tuxedos. Sam and MaryAnne knew all of them and their wives, as Sam had explained earlier, so there shouldn't be any excessive hanky-panky (whatever that meant, Penny thought). The two slightly older ones, Joe and Jack, seemed to attach themselves to Sam and MaryAnne. The taller of the other two, Oliver, had zeroed in on Suzy. That left Penny with Steven, which he didn't seem to mind. They picked up their drinks and toasted the evening to come.

They went to find their table, which had seating for sixteen. The other four couples were, Penny thought, husbands and wives. They were introduced, but by the time they took their seats Penny couldn't remember their names.

The whole table was ready for a fun evening and quickly got into the mood. The girls had been in the mood for five days and had not yet got rid of their giggles. More champagne set them off again. Every time Penny looked at Suzy, Suzy would seductively run her hands down her sides and onto her thighs and give a Marilyn Monroe pucker and Penny would burst into laughter.

Penny couldn't explain it to Steven. She was sure he thought he had landed a psycho. Fortunately they all found something in common to talk about.

When Steven found out that Penny was a prosecuting attorney, he said his practice was in a small town and at times he would fill in as the coroner. He went on to talk about some of his cases and went into detail about a couple of them. She told him that she was only three years out of law school, but working in the DA's office she was given responsibility sooner than if she was with a private firm. She explained that during her first two years, she was an assistant prosecutor and did research. She sat at the prosecutor's table during the trial and provided information for the prosecutor, took notes, and asked questions when she noticed anything unusual. In the last year she had prosecuted a number of cases on her own, mainly DUIs, B&E, some felonies, and assault cases. Most were pretty much open and shut, but they provided good practice in courtroom technique. She told him her real interest was in white collar crime.

They had a pleasant discussion and the meal passed quickly. When the meal was over, the chairman of the conference stood up. Expecting a long talk, they were pleasantly surprised when he announced, "Thanks to all who made this a successful conference and thank you all for coming. This conference is concluded. Have fun and have a safe trip home." It was probably the largest ovation of the entire conference.

The waiters were clearing the tables and the band began to play. It was the moment she had dreaded. She had never been much of a dancer, so during her last year of law school she decided that this moment would come and she should at least prepare for it. She had taken ballroom dancing and felt she wouldn't completely embarrass herself. As someone who walked in a courtroom to take on older and oftentimes wiser defense attorneys without any doubt of her capability, she had a hard time understanding her fear.

Steve turned and offered her his hand. This was the moment of truth. She took his hand and they headed to the dance floor. Steve was an excellent dancer and it was easy to follow him. They made it through that dance and another slow one.

The next one was a waltz, her favorite in dance school. Her first thought was "Oh, they'll be able to see my pretty slip." They did as the couple swirled around the floor, Penny now feeling completely relaxed and thoroughly enjoying herself. The waltz ended and they started playing a cha-cha. Fortunately that was not one of Steve's favorites, so they returned to their table. As she got to her seat Penny looked up to see Sam and MaryAnne smiling, giving her a visual thumbs up. They talked and danced some more.

The girls had talked about going to a late show at some nightclub. When they told their escorts, they were all for it and started discussing places to go, maybe someplace in Pigalle.

Suzy told them of a local club that had a show and was not a tourist trap. They told the concierge where they wanted to go and how many were going. He called two cabs that carried four each. Being the smallest, Penny was given the jump seat. Steve gallantly offered her his lap. She declined. It was a gay group in search of fun.

They arrived at a plain building with a blank wall and a small sign over a nondescript door. The sign simply said "MiMi." They got out and Steve opened the door. They entered a small dark hall. At the end, a heavy drape kept out the light on the other side and muffled the sound. Going through the drapes was entering another world: lights were blinking all over, a band was playing, and there was a low murmur of people talking. Fortunately there was no smoking.

They were shown to the edge of the dance floor where two tables had been put together. They all sat down and discussed the big question, what to drink. They'd had champagne and wine at dinner. Some voted for wine, some for champagne, and one for the hard stuff. Since there was no consensus, they ordered individually. Penny decided to continue with white wine, which she could sip for a long time; she was already feeling giddy from her previous drinks. As they waited for their drinks, they danced to some sultry French music. Steven held her a little closer than she liked, but she was too relaxed to complain; however, when his hand slowly slid down her back toward her butt, she told him he would muss her lace and he got the message. When they returned to the table, the drinks were there.

Just as they sat down, the stage lit up and the master of ceremonies came on and rattled on in French, occasionally speaking to their group in English. He did this throughout the show, so even though they could not follow everything, at least they knew what was going on. He introduced a female singer, very attractive and wearing a gorgeous dress.

She had a throaty voice reminiscent of another French singer. She started her song and out came a line of beautifully almost-dressed women. About half of them were topless; Penny thought she heard Steve take a big breath. They danced and paraded and finally came off the stage and onto the dance floor, passing by their tables. That was when men became little boys, Penny thought. They could hardly sit in their seats. It was amazing how men reacted to two mounds of flesh. Admittedly they were beautiful, although at least half had had help.

When they finished, the MC introduced a comedian. Although all of the girls had some knowledge of French, only Suzy was fluent enough to follow a comedian. She would whisper in Oliver's ear and he would laugh. They became a focus for the comedian.

Penny got the jest that when he told a joke and the audience roared and their group sat there gazing into space, he pointed to them and said something like, "Some people you just can't please," and he got another big laugh out of the audience. Watching Suzy, Penny knew that he really was funny. When he finished, he came over to their table and, talking through Suzy, thanked them for being good sports and for being there. As he left their table, he pointed to them and said something that caused the rest of the audience to give them a hand.

Next there was a ballroom-dancing couple. They performed so gracefully together. They made Penny feel inadequate. A male singer then sang a French love song and the female singer returned. Penny noticed that Steve sat more upright. Again there were many bare bosoms, and the dancers paraded again. This time a couple of them stopped and sat on the men's laps. Penny thought, they'll be telling stories in surgery and in the locker room at the club for the next six months. The show finished with an Apache dance. She turned to Steve and told him not to get any ideas. The lights came on and they ordered another round of drinks. Oliver asked her to dance. She held out her hand and kiddingly said, "As long as you keep your hands to yourself."

Without hesitation, he quipped, "Suzy didn't mind."

This got him a smile and a swat on the back. He wasn't as good a dancer as Steven, but he didn't hold her as tight and they were able to have a pleasant dance.

They started back and Steven intercepted them. He said they had decided this was the last dance and he wanted to have it with Penny. She was touched and followed him onto the dance floor. It was nice, slow, romantic song. Once again he held her closer than she liked, but it was the last dance and he had been very nice and got her through her first real ball. She relaxed and actually put her head on his shoulder. The dance ended and the girls pardoned themselves and went to the ladies' room. They finished by checking their makeup and looking at some puffy eyes. The drive home was in a normal cab and she was forced to sit on Steve's lap. He had his arms around her but behaved himself all the way back.

At the hotel they thanked the boys and said goodnight with a kiss on the cheek. It was decided that Suzy would spend the night since it was so late. MaryAnne was so tired she went straight to bed. Suzy and Penny sat on the couch discussing the evening. Sam came out and saw them talking and decided she would sleep in

MaryAnne's room so Penny wouldn't wake her when she came to bed. Penny and Suzy decided they would talk in bed, so they turned off the lights and went to bed. Penny told Suzy how much she had enjoyed her visit and thanked Suzy for making it so pleasant. She told her that when she came home she should come down to stay at Penny's beach house, that it was a painter's paradise. Suzy grunted, and Penny didn't know if that was a yes or a no or a maybe. Suzy was asleep. Penny rolled over and thought over all the events of the week. She thought she had learned a lot about herself. She drifted off to sleep.

SATURDAY

Penny awoke and found that Suzy was cuddled up against her and had an arm around her. Not wanting to wake her, Penny just lay there feeling very warm and contented. She was a little sad because they would be going home that day, although it was always good to be home. Suzy woke up slowly, and she tried to get closer. It was a little cold in the room.

She grunted and then said, "Good morning. What time is it?"

"A quarter till seven, you want to get up?"

"Not yet. This feels warm and nice. Can we wait until seven?"

Penny reached for her arm and pulled her even closer, feeling the comfort of her body heat. They both went back to sleep. She heard MaryAnne's voice and she came into the room.

"Well, look at the sleepyheads all warm and cuddly," she yelled. "Want me to pull off the covers so you feel that nice cold Paris air?"

They both woke up and grabbed the covers.

"Sam and I are going to breakfast as soon as she gets up and ready. You two are invited," she said as she left the room. They both slid down under the covers to find the warm spot and huddled together.

Finally, Penny said, "Well I feel like I could stay here forever, but I guess it's now or never." She jumped out of bed and threw on her robe and headed for the bathroom.

She thought about Suzy having to go home wearing her gown from last night. She could imagine people looking at Suzy and wondering where she had spent the night, not that it would bother her. She saw Suzy open her purse and pull out a black silk T-shirt and something that was about the size of a small salami. She starting shaking it and it became a long crinkle skirt.

Suzy smiled. "I was a girl scout, so I'm always prepared."

With that they all finished dressing and went down to breakfast. Of course, the conversation was about the previous evening. Each told how she kept her date in line. Sam said that every time he looked as if he wanted to get frisky, she would talk about his wife. She said it took a while, but he finally got the message, and he was quite the gentleman the rest of the evening.

MaryAnne said her date was so well behaved she started to have doubts about her desirability. They all knew how sexy she looked and provided no sympathy.

Suzy's story, told with sighs and giggles, was about her date taking every opportunity to brush against her bosom. "I thought he was going to wear through the material. It reminded me of a junior high dance. I almost told him to grab a handful and get it over with once and for all. I really didn't mind. I thought it was kinda cute. He touched me with every part of his hand and arm and excused himself each time. I think he will remember that night and embellish each time he thinks about it."

There was silence and they all looked at Penny. She would have preferred to just listen, but it was obvious that they wouldn't let her get by without providing some tidbit. So she told them about Steven allowing his hand to slide down her back toward her butt and telling him that he would mess up her lace, and that he behaved the rest of the evening. They just stared and finally burst out laughing.

"You really told him that? That he would mess up your lace?" they questioned.

"Well, it worked!" she replied and sat back with a smug look on her face.

They decided to take one last trip to Notre Dame Cathedral. Penny lit candles for her parents and said a short prayer. They walked around and ended up at the entrance. Sam ask where they would like to eat their last meal in Paris. MaryAnne suggested the Frog and Pickle.

Sam looked at her. "We would need a reservation to get in, especially on a Saturday." Penny agreed. Suzy didn't say anything, but looked a little suspicious.

MaryAnne said, "If I can get us in, then you pay, bet?"

Sam was now suspicious, but it was worth the chance, "OK, you're on."

When they got to the restaurant, the expected long line was there.

"Well, do we find a McDonald's?" joked Sam.

MaryAnne stepped forward. "Oh, you of little faith, let me whip out my southern charm and I will get us a table!" She walked up to the gentleman taking requests and spoke to him; an expression of glee came over his face and he took her arm and started to lead her into the restaurant, and she turned and waved to her friends to come on in. As they reached her, she whispered to Sam, "Hope you have your best credit card, I'm hungry."

As the ladies walked in past the waiting line, Suzy nudged Penny. "This is not a surprise to MaryAnne."

They were met inside by the maître d', who had been there on the night MaryAnne assisted the lady who was choking. He was falling all over himself to serve. He led them to a special table in the most desirable section of the dining room.

"May I suggest our special menu for the day?"

Without consulting the others, MaryAnne said, "That will be fine, thank you."

Sam just sat there looking at MaryAnne; this meal could run into real money. When MaryAnne picked up and started to peruse the wine list, even Penny started getting apprehensive.

"The Duchess said if you returned, you were to be served from her wine cellars, and if you like, I will choose for you. She has one of the finest cellars here," said the maître d'. It became obvious that the meal had been planned and was a gift from the Duchess.

They all looked at MaryAnne, who sat there with a very smug look on her face. The only one not surprised was Suzy. She whispered, "Remember, I told you she was up to something!"

There were two waiters serving, and the maître d' hovered around checking that all was well. After going through the whole menu, they were four stuffed ladies. They thanked everyone and assured the maître d' they would tell the Duchess of the wonderful meal and the outstanding service they had received. MaryAnne and the maître d's conversation was filled with "merci's".

The four returned to the hotel for final packing. In the lobby, Suzy said she had to go. She had things she needed to get done. They all stood to say their good-byes. The others gave her hugs and kisses, as women do, and said how happy they were to have met her and they hoped to see her again. When she turned to Penny, Penny felt her eyes grow moist and she gave Suzy a big hug and a kiss.

"Thanks, and I hope you come to Florida sometimes" was all she could say.

Suzy's answer was, "I enjoyed your visit very much. I'll see if I can."

Another hug and a kiss and she was gone. Although Penny had only known her four days, she felt an emptiness when she was gone. In those short four days she had become a dear friend.

They went to their suite to finish packing and get ready for their flight back home. Penny had purchased an inexpensive, small bag—just to carry her new dress, some other clothing, and some gifts she had bought. Her new dress was the last item she packed.

While she was carefully folding it, "Careful not to mess the lace!" came from the other side of room, accompanied by snickers and giggles. She gave them a very unladylike finger and stuck her tongue out at them. And she thought how lucky she was to have such close friends that they could tease each other like they did and enjoy it. Yes, those two were special.

On the trip home, their spirits were not as high as when they came, even after a martini in the lounge. The champagne on the plane helped, but all in all, it was a subdued flight home. When the plane touched down at the airport, Penny had the usual mixed feelings of ending a vacation and being home. The passage through passport control and customs was quick and uneventful. Since they lived reasonably close to one another, the women were able to take the same cab. Penny was the last to get home.

The apartment was dark and quiet. She turned on the lights, and the familiar surroundings were comforting. It was late, so she only took out and hung up her new dress, after standing in front of her mirror and holding it up to get one last look before putting it away. She relived the farewell party and wondered when she would have the opportunity to wear the dress again. She undressed, showered, put on a nightie, and got ready for bed. But first she checked her e-mail: thirty-three of them. She looked for any needing immediate action, but none did, and she went to bed. Fortunately, the next day was not a work day, so she could sleep late and unpack. It was the end of a wonderful week.

Chapter Sixteen

BACK TO WORK

It was tough to get up and go to work after an exciting week in Paris, but life must go on, and Max had told Penny she had a new case for her.

During her shower, she thought about what the case would be. Realizing she had no scheduled appointments for the day, she declared it a dress down day.

Finishing her shower, she put on her underwear and one of her new bras from Paris. She rummaged through her closet until she found a pair of old worn jeans and put those on. She completed her outfit with a University of Miami T-shirt. Brushing her hair and putting it in a ponytail, she finished by applying a little makeup and some lipstick. She look in the mirror and saw a little girl looking back at her. She smiled and thought, maybe someday I'll grow up. She grabbed a bag containing a scarf she had gotten for Max and left for work.

Max was at her desk working on the paperwork that she tried to finish first thing in the morning. She looked up and saw Penny, and without even a smile, she said, "Sorry, young lady, you have to be at least eighteen to work here," and looked down at her work. She jumped up and grabbed Penny and gave her a big hug, whispering, "Girl, it's great to see you, and welcome back. You can tell me all about Paris when we have dinner at your place this weekend."

Penny smiled. She hadn't thought about having a dinner party, but it would a good way for everyone to get together and talk about their adventure. She also knew that Max meant they didn't have time right now for anything but work.

Max began, "Sit down, Penny, we have a case of a union rep and a city council member making a deal. We have it on tape, the whole transaction."

"Should be open and shut."

"Yeah, that's what I thought until I found out the union was bringing in a couple of high-powered lawyers."

"I never knew you to worry about big-time lawyers. Are these two special?"

"No, but I've got a feeling that there is something about the warrant that may allow them to prohibit using the tape. They seem awfully confident. When you walked in, I thought, maybe we can make them overconfident. One of their lawyers is due here at nine-thirty to trade witness lists and discuss scheduling, etcetera. I want you to review the case and return it by nine-fifteen. I'm going to tell him that it looks like a simple case and that since I have several more important cases, I'm assigning one of my junior prosecutors to this one. That's you. You're dressed for the occasion. No one looking at you would think you're capable of prosecuting a major case. Just be the sweet young thing you are, and he'll be hooked. Then we figure out how to win this case."

Penny took the case file and returned to her office to study it. She finished and returned the file to Max.

"We'll talk later after our turkey leaves," Max said, and waved her off.

At 9:40 a.m. Max called and Penny went to her office. Max introduced the lawyer as a Mr. Robert Lee from Chicago. Penny went through her routine, apologizing and trying to explain her attire. She seemed perplexed when Max told her that she was assigned the case. Max explained she had discussed the scheduling and had exchanged the potential witness list.

"You will see that he has access to whatever he requests. From here on, he will contact you directly in all matters concerning this case," said Max. "Give him your card and you can start reviewing the case, OK? Nice to meet you, Mr. Lee, I leave you in good hands." She turned back to her desk indicating the meeting was over.

Penny led Lee back to her office. She walked and skipped like a teenager. Lee just smiled and shook his head. He handed her a list of items to which he wanted access. She noted that the videotape was first on the list. She looked and fussed and finally said she would check and contact him in a couple of days. He smiled, thanked her, and offered his hand in saying good-bye. As soon as he left, Penny headed for Max's office.

Max was sitting there with her feet on her desk and a big smile on her face. "Well, I think he left here thinking this office was full of lunatics."

"Yeah, and I'm the teenage queen nut," Penny quipped. "Now, how do we win this case?"

"It's your case, honey, that's your problem."

"Thanks. Feinstein is the investigator."

Max dropped her feet to the floor and turned in her chair. "Captain Feinstein, newly promoted, you know him?"

"I know of him. Everything I've heard has been good. Is he available to me for further assistance?"

"I'll see he's yours as much as you need him," Max said as she picked up her briefcase and started for the door. "Remember, Penny, this is your case, but I'm here for any help I can be, so go study and we'll get together tomorrow." She left and Penny went to her office, grabbed a pen and notepad, and started to work.

She wrote on her pad:

A. Review the videotaping—check warrant

B. Check with Captain Feinstein

1. Evidence taken from treasurer's office

2. Financial records of both treasurer and union official

C. Criminal records of both

D. Check on defense attorneys

E. Check court calendar

F. Review the warrant for the videotaping

She placed a call to Captain Feinstein and asked him if they could get together first thing in the morning and discuss the case. They arranged a time and agreed to meet at her office. She picked up her laptop and headed home.

As soon as she got home, she took off her jeans and T-shirt and put on a robe, sat on the couch, and turned on her laptop. First she Googled the two lawyers, Robert Lee and Bruce Denver; both had graduated from Harvard and had impressive resumes. It appeared that Lee was the junior of the two. They had done extensive work for the union including three similar cases to this one. They had won all three.

She next Googled "Ralph Brown, the union man." He had been a union official for thirteen years and moved through the ranks and was now a union negotiator.

She logged onto the police net and checked for any criminal records for Mr. Brown. He had a history of violence during strikes but was never convicted. His only conviction was for assault and battery against a supervisor eighteen years ago. He was fined and given a suspended sentence.

She Googled Ryan Gilbert, a member of the city council for six years. Prior to that he was a supervisor at the department of transportation, and had no criminal record. She made a note: Have Feinstein check Gilbert's finances.

She turned off her laptop and put it back in its carrying case. She went into the kitchen and made herself a simple salad of tuna from a can, romaine lettuce, dates cut into small pieces, and blue cheese dressing, and topped it off with some croutons. She poured herself a glass of white wine and sat down in front of the TV to watch the evening news. "The weather will continue warm with possible showers." This is Florida, what else is new? A car chase in Miami, an attempted robbery of a convenience store, a cat that traveled twenty-three miles to return home after being trapped in a moving van. Surprisingly, the next was news to Penny. Ralph Brown was standing with two other men. She recognized one as Robert Lee and surmised the other one was his co-council. The local reporter was asking Mr. Brown about his indictment and if he felt it was just.

"I'm sure that it was pressure from the outside that forced the DA's office to take the action it did."

His lawyer, not Lee, stepped in and said that the charges were unfounded and Mr. Brown would be exonerated, that the charges would possibly be dropped before the case went to court.

The program moved on to someone picketing bake sales at a local school, the "News of the day." She turned the news off and watched an old M.A.S.H. rerun. Her thoughts were still on the Brown segment. They seemed sure the videotape would not be allowed as evidence. If it was allowed, the case would be a slam dunk.

Penny's job would be to find out why they felt the tape would be denied as evidence and counteract it or find a different path. She was looking forward to seeing Captain Feinstein and discussing it with him. She called it a night and got ready for bed. Tomorrow was another day.

Tomorrow, which became today, started with her usual glass of grapefruit juice and a two-mile jog. She showered and dressed in her usual day-at-the-office clothing: a gray skirt, a white tailored blouse, and a brown blazer. Since she wouldn't be in court, she wore brown loafers. She stopped at Starbucks for a latte and a muffin, promising that tomorrow she would eat a better breakfast. It wasn't the first time she had made that promise.

She arrived at the office before Max and went to her office to prepare for her meeting with Captain Feinstein. Max arrived shortly after, with a coffee and a Danish, and sat down and started on her Danish. With a full mouth she ask Penny what her plan was. Penny told her that she would talk to Feinstein and see what he had found when he went to Gilbert's office. She was going to see what they had about the summons that would negate using the videotape.

Her meeting with Captain Feinstein proved very productive. The search of Gilbert's office had uncovered a number of tapes recorded by the treasurer. The captain was having the tapes transcribed. It seemed that the warrant to record the treasurer and his visitors had a technical problem and would prevent its use in court. Penny would take an alternate route. The defense seemed to think that without the tape, there was no case! She did love surprises, especially if they were her surprises.

* * *

On the day of the trial, Penny entered the court carrying a Gucci briefcase, dressed as a professional, in a perfectly tailored gray suit and a stark white blouse with just the right amount of ruffles to emphasize femininity. She wore a black cameo brooch with matching earrings. Her hair hung below her shoulders and framed her girlish face, showing her hazel eyes and a bright smile. It didn't show the determination and toughness behind those eyes. Robert Lee, the defense attorney with whom she had worked in the beginning of the case, took one look and declared, mostly to himself, "We've been had, this is not an inexperienced attorney."

He turned to look at his associate, who was now the lead attorney for the defense, to see if he noticed Penny's arrival. He was busy talking with Max, who had come in earlier and would be Penny's co-counselor.

Since he was the junior defense attorney and his partner was not partial to advice, he decided he would let him find out for himself that this might not be as cut and dried as they had thought.

The court was called to order and the judge came in and took his seat. At their attorneys' request, the two defendants were being tried together; both had pleaded "Not guilty."

After going through the formalities, Penny called her first witness, the chief of police.

"Chief, will you explain how this case evolved?"

"The department had received a number of anonymous calls stating the defendants were engaged in fixing contracts so that union organized companies were being awarded contracts without competitive bids or being the lower bidder."

Penny asked, "Is it unusual to receive such calls?"

"No, we constantly get such calls alleging misconduct. We do a preliminary investigation to determine if the allegations warrant further investigation. The sheer number of calls we were receiving about this case was justification to continue our investigation," he said.

Penny's next question was, "What did you do then?"

The chief answered that he placed Captain Feinstein in charge of a task force to fully investigate the allegations.

"Thank you, Chief. Your witness, counselor." Penny sat down.

Bruce Denver, the lead defense attorney, stood up and walked slowly over to the witness. "Chief, do you always investigate anonymous calls even though you don't know who made them?"

"If we knew who made them, they wouldn't be anonymous, but yes, we do make an effort to ascertain the validity of each call," he replied.

The defense attorney, evidently irked by the chief's remark, asked, "And how many such calls do you get in a day or a week?"

"I don't have that on the tip of my tongue, but if it's important, I'll have someone get the info for you."

"How many calls about this particular situation did you receive?"

The chief seemed to concentrate before saying, "Between eight and twelve would be my guess, but I can get the exact number if you desire."

"Do you consider that a large number?"

"On one subject, yes, I think it's a very significant number."

"You said you set up a task force to investigate. Did you think anonymous phone calls dictated that much resources to be expended at that time?"

The chief sat up straight and said, "Sir, I took an oath to protect the citizens of this city, and other than capital crimes I know of no more serious crime than betraying the public trust."

"Thank you, Chief, for your forthrightness and the duty you perform for this community. I have no more questions for this witness, Your Honor." Bruce sat down.

Robert Lee looked at his fellow attorney and thought, "He's not off to a very good start. All he did was antagonize the chief and half the population."

Penny called Captain Feinstein to the stand. After he was sworn in and stated his name and position, Penny asked about any special training he had. He replied that he had a BS in Criminology and a number of courses on special subjects taken locally at the university, including several in accounting, and special courses taught by the FBI.

Penny's next question was, "How did you proceed once you were assigned to the case?"

"Myself and the two sergeants were assigned to the case and began by going over all the contracts let by the city in the last three years. We separated those that were awarded to companies not presenting the lowest bids or which were no bid contracts.

"We analyzed each of those trying to determine the reason why the low bids weren't accepted. There were a number of contracts where we could not determine why. That became the real starting point of the investigation.

"We talked to users of the contracts to be sure there were no extenuating circumstances, such as special equipment or expertise that the lowest bidder couldn't supply, therefore mandating another supplier.

"Going back over contracts the city had let, we found twelve we questioned. Of those twelve, three had been let to either family or close friends or associates of members of the city council. The only commonality of the nine others was they were all let to companies having a strong tie to a local union. Of the nine, only one member had voted every time for the union companies and was one of the persons named a number of times in the anonymous phone calls. We started with him.

"We applied for a warrant to place a video camera in his office to be used if and when the other defendant had an appointment with the city official in question. We also obtained a warrant to gather evidence from the official's office and his home. The second warrant was not executed until after the meeting between the two defendants."

Penny, who was still during the captain's entire testimony, turned and went back to the table and picked up a folder. Slowly opening it, she said, "Let's discuss some of the evidence you found. First the tapes."

Before she could go further, Bruce jumped to his feet and shouted, "Objection, Your Honor. May we approach the bench?" The judge nodded, and Bruce and Penny went before the judge.

Bruce whispered, "Your Honor. I'm for giving this inexperienced young lady a lot of latitude, but even a first-year law student should know you can't introduce evidence the court has declared invalid because of an improper search warrant. Please inform her she can't even mention it."

The judge, looking over the top of his glasses, said, "Well, Ms. Penny, inexperienced counselor, what do you have to say?"

"I don't know what he's talking about, Your Honor. Which tape?" she asked in a voice that was definitely not a whisper. "If the learned and experienced counselor will let me proceed, he'll learn that there's more than 'The Tape' involved in this case, and I was referring to one of the twenty-seven tapes removed from the defendant's office."

The look on Bruce's face showed he was not aware of the significance of the other tapes.

The judge looked at Bruce and said, "Well, counselor, shall we let the young lady continue?"

"Yes, Your Honor." Bruce hurried back to his table. He leaned over and asked Lee what he knew about the other tapes. Lee just shrugged his shoulders. He was starting to enjoy the show.

Penny spoke: "If the defense is through discussing its problems, I would like to continue, and I will try to spoil your day."

"Ms. Penny, please limit your remarks to the court and get on with your examination." The judge sounded harsh, but there was a small smile on his face.

Penny made a slight bow to the judge and said, "Thank you, Your Honor." Turning to the witness, she said, "Let's discuss the tapes you found in the defendant's office. How many were there?"

"There were over fifty, counting the country and western ones, but we were interested in twenty-seven. Twenty had been completely recorded, one was partially used, and the others were blank. All of these tapes had been new and only used one time."

"Is this important?" interjected Penny.

"Yes, as it turned out. Because parts of the tapes had been erased only once, that simplifies the restoration of information that had been taped before."

"Is that possible?" asked Penny.

"In many cases, yes," continued the captain. "We made a preliminary reading of the tapes and found the tapes contained recordings of Mr. Gilbert and his visitors. However, some portions of some of the tapes were erased."

"Before we get into the information on the tapes, can you tell us how they were recorded?" Penny asked.

"Mr. Gilbert had a very elaborate recording system that was voice controlled. That is, it would be started by a sound of sufficient amplitude to trigger the unit.

"It would continue as long as someone was talking or for five additional minutes if there was no more sound. It would automatically start again when someone spoke. It was also programmed to mark the date at the beginning of each day, and to mark each hour."

Penny turned and walked back to her table and picked up another folder. Opening the folder and glancing through a couple of pages, she asked, "Then it would be possible to connect the conversations with the individual, if you had Mr. Gilbert's appointment schedule?"

"Yes, that's correct," responded the captain.

Penny paused and then asked, "Did you find his schedule?"

The captain moved a little to get more comfortable and answered, "Yes, we found his schedule on his computer, but all the appointments scheduled for the times when the tapes in question were made had been deleted. We checked his secretary's appointment schedule, and all of her computer files had been deleted."

"What did Mrs. Crowley have to say about that?" inquired Penny.

"Mrs. Crowley retired two days before the search warrant was issued and immediately took sixty days of accumulated leave and is now on a cruise somewhere in Asia," the captain said. "She is due back in a couple of weeks."

Penny looked over at the defense table and saw Gilbert with a smirk on his face and thought, you'll remove that smirk in a moment. She turned and said, "Does that mean, Captain, that we cannot ascertain the individuals in those conversations that were erased?"

Looking at Gilbert, the captain replied, "No, being a very efficient secretary, Mrs. Crowley, in addition to keeping them on her computer, had all of his appointments in a notebook she kept in a file. Fortunately the replacement secretary had not gotten around to cleaning out all the files."

Penny again looked at the defense table; the smirk was replaced by a look of apprehension. Penny once more went to her table and returned with a tan notebook. She handed it to Feinstein and asked him if he recognized it.

"Yes, it is the notebook we found in Mr. Gilbert's office. My initials are on the back."

The defense attorney jumped to his feet and said, "Objection, Your Honor, I was not made aware of that notebook or its contents and it should not be allowed as evidence in this case."

"Well, Ms. Penny, what do you say?"

"Your Honor, the notebook is listed along with all the other material removed from Mr. Gilbert's office, and the list was made available to the defense. He had access to anything we had. We can only make it available, we can't force him to take it and read it."

The judge, in a mild reprimand, said, "Counselors, I am only interested in facts, not opinions. The objection is overruled."

"Sorry, Your Honor," Penny said as she turned back to Captain Feinstein and asked, "Can you determine who the participants are during the erased period from entries in the notebook?"

"Yes, of course. Mr. Gilbert was one party in all of the conversations. There were three others involved, a Mr. Henk, a local contractor; a Mr. Beagle, another contractor; and the defendant, Mr. Brown. The first two were only in one conversation, Mr. Brown was in the others."

"Have you recovered all the conversations?" Penny asked.

"No. We have transcribed four, the two with the contractors and the last two with Mr. Brown. If necessary, we'll do the rest."

"Why only four?" asked Penny.

"It's a time-consuming task and ties up a lot of assets that are needed elsewhere. If the other transcriptions are needed then we can apply to have them done."

Penny turned to the judge and said, "Your Honor, I would like to excuse this witness for now but recall him later."

The judge nodded and Penny turned to Bruce. "Your witness."

"Captain, have you read the transcripts?" Bruce asked.

"Yes."

"Do you think the others should be transcribed?"

"Sir, I'm a detective. I only gather facts, I don't give opinions."

Bruce hesitated and then asked, "Captain, when you entered the notebook on the list of items you removed from the defendant's office, do you think that listing it as just a brown secretarial notebook was sufficient identification for an item that the prosecution is using as primary evidence?"

Feinstein shrugged his shoulders and replied, "When we removed the notebook, that's just all it was, Mrs. Crowley's notebook."

Bruce, with a grin on his face as if he had caught his son's hand in the cookie jar, asked, "Wouldn't it have been clearer if you had entered the item as 'Mrs. Crowley's notebook' instead of trying to hide its real value by tagging it as just a notebook?"

Feinstein gave Bruce a look of disgust before answering, "First, as I said at the time, it was just a brown secretarial notebook. Secondly, it was listed under items that were removed from Mrs. Crowley's file cabinet. I wouldn't think you have to be a detective to figure out that it was Mrs. Crowley's."

Bruce turned to the judge, but before he had a chance to speak, the judge spoke: "The witness will just answer the question and will not editorialize." Anyone looking closely would have seen a twinkle in his eyes. "Continue."

"Captain, are you aware that, in Florida, to legally record a conversation, both parties must be knowledgeable that the recording is taking place?" asked Bruce.

"Yes, and I assumed Mr. Gilbert was also."

"Did you ask him?"

"No. After we read him his rights, his lawyer instructed him to answer no more questions."

A low level of chuckles echoed through the courtroom. The judge looked up with a stern expression on his face and the chuckles quickly dissipated.

Bruce hesitated and asked if he could approach the bench. The judge nodded, and Bruce and Penny went up. Bruce asked the judge for a short recess. He needed to confer with his clients. The judge agreed and banged his gavel. "The jury will be removed to the jury room for a thirty-minute recess." When they had left he banged his gavel again: "The court will recess for fifteen minutes."

Bruce left with his clients and his associates to go to a conference room. "All right, you assholes, you assured me that all they had was the videotape that I successfully had removed as evidence. Now it seems that not only did they have audiotapes of your conversations, but ones Gilbert made himself."

Gilbert stuttered, "But I erased those parts, how was I to know they could be read?"

Brown was fuming. "You shit, you thought you had to record my meetings with you, trying to cover your ass, or maybe blackmail! You ..."

Evidently he couldn't think of an appropriate epithet and sat back in his chair with a scowl on his face.

"Can't you get the tapes thrown out? Don't all parties have to know they're being taped? And I didn't know," said Brown.

"Did you ever sign in when you came to my office?" asked Gilbert.

"I may have, the first or second time, but not after that, although your secretary gave me a hard time because I didn't. So what?" said Brown.

"On the sign-in sheet there was a paragraph in small print stating that all discussions in my office would be recorded. The guy who sold me the equipment told me about the law and recommended that I add that paragraph to a sign-in sheet. If you signed in, then you acknowledge that the conversations were being recorded."

"Since Gilbert recorded your conversation, I can't represent you both. It would be a conflict of interest. We could possibly get a new trial for each of you separately, but with the evidence they have, I don't think there is any way both of you wouldn't be convicted," explained Bruce.

Brown, stone faced, said, "Well, so, what are we going to do?"

"I'm not sure what I'm going to do, but you two are probably going to jail," said Bruce. "OK, I'll represent you, and Bob will represent Gilbert. We will go and talk to the prosecution team and see what terms we can negotiate. Is that OK with the two of you?"

"Since he recorded me without my permission, can't we get those tapes thrown out?" asked Brown.

Lee explained. "Two things. I checked and the Eleventh Circuit says there are two exceptions, one regarding recording police officers in performance of their duties, and two, recording public officials in performing their duties in public places. If you signed those registers, then you said you knew you would be recorded. We could try that approach and may even get a new trial, but I believe, in the end, the outcome would be the same. I think we can plea bargain a better deal now.

"What we need to do now is to decide how to minimize your sentence."

Gilbert actually sobbed.

"We'll go back in and we'll talk to the prosecutor and see what we can negotiate," Bruce continued. "It means you'll have to plead guilty. Then, depending how we can plea bargain and how kind the prosecutor is, they will decide on the sentence."

Bruce led the group back into the courtroom, and as soon as the judge returned he went to the bench and requested a meeting between himself and the prosecutors. Bruce, Lee, and a local attorney for the defense met with Penny and Max, for the prosecution.

Bruce started, "We would like to find out what kind of sentence our clients might receive if they decided to plead guilty."

Penny and Max had discussed this when it became apparent that the defendants would be found guilty.

Penny replied, "Guidelines are from five to twenty years. We would recommend only the minimum jail time of five years with two conditions. First a fine of one hundred and twenty-five thousand dollars each—that's the amount of money we figured the city lost—and a condition that neither of them work in any government position or participate in any union activities during their probation period, which we recommend to be a minimum of fifteen years."

The judge asked, "Well, Mr. Denver, would you like to consult with your clients?"

Bruce got up from his chair and said, "I would," and they all trooped out.

At the defense table, Bruce explained the terms.

Brown exploded. "That young bitch wants to send us to jail for five years?"

"Watch your language," Bruce snapped. "That young lady could have demanded a much longer sentence. The only question is, do you both want to accept?"

Gilbert asked, "What do you suggest?"

"I think we ought to accept," Bruce replied. "If we continued with the trial and lost, with the evidence the DA has, the sentence would probably be greater."

Brown said, "Great, we get two Harvard graduates and they let a young Florida Cracker bitch clean their clock. So it appears we have no choice. OK, I'll plead guilty, let's get it over with."

Bruce turned to Gilbert. "You?"

Gilbert, unable to talk, just nodded his head.

The three defense lawyers met with the prosecution team and agreed to the sentence. They then they conferred with the judge, who approved it.

"OK, when the judge comes back, he'll ask if you want to change your plea. You'll say yes and plead guilty." Bruce went back to the chambers and confirmed his clients were ready to change their pleas.

The judge reconvened the court and explained to the jury the defendants had changed their plea to guilty and their job was concluded. He thanked them for performing their civic duties and dismissed the jury. He then had the defendants rise, and he pronounced the sentence agreed upon. The court business was concluded.

The bailiff said, "All rise."

As the judge started to leave the courtroom, he caught Penny's eye. He winked and smiled, just a little.

As the courtroom started to clear, Lee came over to Penny, offered his hand, and said, "You're an even better attorney than you are an actress." He smiled and left before she could answer.

While Penny and Max were clearing up all the paper on the table, Bruce stopped by to congratulate them on their performance and then quickly left. Penny and Max looked at each other. They were happy they had won, but neither was happy to see people go to jail, even if they deserved it, as these two certainly did.

As they made their way toward the courthouse exit, they were continually being stopped to be congratulated. When they finally left the building, Max said, "I need peace and quiet and a drink, how about you?"

"Yes, and I know just the place," said Penny. "Dr. Taylor is about to have happy hour right about now, and she is going to have guests." A quick phone call, and they were on their way.

Chapter Seventeen

SUZY

Penny picked up her mail from the floor beneath the mail slot and sorted through it: an ad, a bill, another bill, a charitable request, more bills, and a letter postmarked Maine. Her mail became instantly more interesting. She hadn't heard from Suzy in a couple of months. Eagerly opening the envelope, she was pleased to read that Suzy was coming for a visit, maybe an extended visit. Suzy had been living in Maine with her family while she traveled around painting.

Penny began to make plans: first, a small welcoming party with Suzy's old friends Sam and MaryAnne and new friends Max and David. They would have the party at the beach house.

Penny used the beach house occasionally on weekends and had not used it for several weeks. She would take a long weekend and clean. Suzy would arrive the following Friday, and they would have the party on Saturday.

* * *

Penny arrived at the airport an hour early, parked in short term parking, and went to the bar to wait. When the plane's arrival was announced, Penny went to the baggage claim area. As she watched passengers come down the escalator, she noticed the different styles of dress: most were exceedingly casual, this being Florida, while a few women wore dresses and a few men wore suits.

When she saw Suzy, she wasn't sure where she fit. She wore a red skirt, very short, with black tights and a black silk turtleneck. She was striking and very attractive.

Suzy saw her at about the same time. They ran to greet each other, tightly embracing and giving each other a more than friendly kiss. When they separated they just looked at each other for an instant. They both took a deep breath and hugged again. Suzy got her bags, and hand in hand they walked to Penny's car. They talked all the way to the condo.

As soon as they took Suzy's luggage inside, they hugged and kissed. Penny said, "I missed you so much. How long can you stay?"

"How long can you put up with me?" asked Suzy.

"You'll be here forever," Penny responded.

They went into the living room. Penny poured each a glass of white wine, and they snuggled on the couch to watch the news.

Neither was aware of what the commentator had to say. They just relaxed in each other's arms. They stayed that way until bedtime. Penny told Suzy about the party and the beach house. Suzy suggested they go out in the morning and get everything ready.

Suzy took her shower first and was in bed when Penny had finished hers. Penny put on her nightie. It was white silk with a lacy bodice. As Suzy saw her, she remembered Penny's love of lacy slips, and guessed it carried over to her nighties. Penny climbed into bed. Suzy put her arm around her, and they cuddled up. Suzy almost immediately fell asleep. She had had a full day traveling.

Penny lay beside her, feeling the warmth of her body, totally content.

* * *

Penny woke first. They had rolled over during the night and Penny was cuddled against Suzy's back. Her hand was lying on Suzy's stomach. Penny slowly moved her hand up, stirred by the velvet feeling of Suzy's skin. She stopped as she reached Suzy's breast. As she lay there, she felt Suzy's hand grab hers and move it to encompass her breast. Neither moved. Suzy went back to sleep and Penny lay there not wanting to move.

Penny finally got up, careful not to wake Suzy. She dressed in her running togs, drank her grapefruit juice, and went for her two-mile run. She stopped on her way back and picked up bagels and cream cheese. When she arrived home, Suzy was just waking up. Penny put the bagels in the kitchen and went in to take a shower. Suzy was lying there, not moving but with her eyes open. Penny leaned over and kissed her. "Get up, it's a new day."

"You're not this happy every day, are you?" asked Suzy.

"No, but your being here makes me happy. Now get up."

After her shower, Penny went into the kitchen and found Suzy had made coffee and had the bagels in the toaster. She wore yellow shorts and a SCAD (Savanna College of Art and Design) T-shirt, loafers, and a big smile.

Over breakfast they decided to have a barbecue at the beach house. Penny would prepare the steaks and Suzy would provide the salad and a casserole. They made a list of what they would need. They would buy it all on the way down.

This was Suzy's first visit to the beach house and she was enthralled. The palms, the oaks, and the citrus trees, a forest through which you got a glimpse of the blue ocean. As she walked through the trees, the surf became more visible and the roar became louder. Penny was right behind her. The sun was bright and hot.

Suzy stopped and said, "I hereby declare Tipen beach topless for today." She then reached around and pulled the string holding up her bikini top and threw the top in the air. Penny hesitated a moment, removed her top, and threw it in the air. The two of them looked at each other, laughed, and ran into the surf. They chased each other and rode the surf. Finally exhausted, they ran onto the beach and flopped on the sand.

Later, Penny stood up and started back to the house. Just as they got there, MaryAnne arrived. She stared at the two, topless and grinning.

Suzy yelled, "This beach has been declared topless for the day." They grabbed MaryAnne and pulled her shirt off. "Topless means no bra either."

MaryAnne reached around, unhooked her bra, and removed it. "Welcome, Suzy. I see things are going to be lively now that you are here."

She went to Suzy and hugged her, nipple to nipple, so to speak. The three of them had a group hug.

"Well, what can I do to help?" MaryAnne asked as she started toward the house.

Suzy answered, "You can help put together the salad. We just have to put the casserole and the potatoes in the oven and marinate the steaks. We can open the wine and let it breathe. The beer is in the cooler and iced down. The tables are set up and the plates and silverware are on the table. That's about it for now. Let's go to the beach for a while."

They left a note:
At the beach.
The beach today is declared TOPLESS.
Penny
MaryAnne
Suzy

"Sam and David should be the next to come," Penny said. "I've always wanted to surprise David. He'll probably look and say something like 'Aren't you girls getting cold?'"

They went to the beach and were sitting facing the surf when they heard someone approaching the beach.

They ignored whoever it was and continued talking. Then they heard "I hope you ladies are covered with suntan lotion. Nothing is more uncomfortable then wearing a bra over well-done breasts."

They all turned and got up at the same time. There stood Sam, topless. David didn't want to remove his shirt, and he'd stayed in the house. Another group hug and they all sat down and started to talk.

Above the chatter, they heard a male voice say, "Curiosity got the better of me. Hello, ladies." They all jumped up, covering their breasts with their hands, even Sam. "You do know that if you're going to fix dinner, you are going to have to lower your hands," laughed David.

All four ladies dropped their hands, and David blushed. He sat down and they talked some more. Suzy told them about her travels around the country, painting. She had spent time in New England, mostly along the coast painting the seashore. She went to Arizona to paint the desert and to California to paint the giant redwoods. She said she was ready to settle down for a while.

"Time to get ready for dinner," said Suzy. They all got up and started toward the house. As they got off the beach, the ladies starting putting on T-shirts. The only one yet to arrive was Max, as she was working late. She drove in just as they got to the house. She jumped out and kissed all around, and asked, "Did I miss anything?"

"Just David ogling a bunch of tits," Sam said casually. David tried to reply but was drowned out by laughter.

They finished preparing the dinner and ate it sitting around a campfire. The wine and conversation flowed freely, until the moon was as high as some of the guests. As they staggered off to bed, Suzy reminded them that tomorrow was also topless. For some reason, they all looked at David.

The next morning, all wearing T-shirts, they had a pickup breakfast. After cleaning up, all except Penny, Suzy, and David left for the beach, removing their tops as soon as they reached the beach area. David was still sitting and drinking his coffee. He ask if he could help, and they told him he could fill the ice chest with ice and cold drinks of all kinds. The ice chest was on the back of a golf cart used to transport people and refreshments to the beach.

While he was completing that task, Penny and Suzy made sandwiches and side dishes, enough to hold them over until dinner. They all got in the golf cart and David headed for the beach. When they got to the beach perimeter, the girls took off their T-shirts and looked at David. "Well?"

He stopped the cart and removed his shirt. "If it makes you happy." As he was wearing dark sunglasses, they couldn't see any expression on his face, just a small dimple at the edge of his mouth. He was having a ball.

Chapter Eighteen

PUPPIES

The next weekend, Penny loaded up her car with a gift for Suzy, plus accessories, and headed to the beach house. As she drove in, she saw the sign had been changed to "TOPLESS." Suzy was just coming back from the beach and she was following her rules: she was topless. That is, she didn't have a garment covering her breasts, but she definitely had quite a top.

Seeing her like that always gave Penny a thrill. She parked the car, got out, and hugged Suzy. She gave her a big kiss and led her to the back of the car. As she hit the button that would open the hatchback, she said, "Surprise." There was a large box and it was rocking. First a black nose appeared, followed by two paws, followed by two more paws and another black nose. Suzy squealed and picked up a squirming Doberman puppy. Penny picked up the other one and they took them over to patio.

Penny, trying hold a squirming pup, said, "Didn't want you to get lonesome. And in a few months, they'll keep unwanted people from bothering you."

Suzy responded, "I've been thinking about a pet, but you made the right choice, I just love them."

Penny got up and took her pup back to the car. Suzy followed with hers. "I brought a small enclosure that will hold them until you can decide what type of fencing you'll need."

They set up the fencing and put in food, water, and the puppies. They sat and just watched the puppies play.

"Oh, I love them so much. Thank you! What should we name them?" said Suzy.

"How about next weekend we have a 'name the puppies party'?"

Suzy clapped her hands like a little kid. "Sounds like fun. You invite and I'll delight," she laughed.

Later that day they took the puppies down to the beach. When they got to the beach, Suzy removed her top and playfully shook it at a puppy, which immediately grabbed one end and began a game of tug-of-war. Suzy dropped the other end and the other puppy grabbed it and the two began a fight over it.

The material was flimsy and in no time the pups had destroyed half of it. Penny laughed when she envisioned Suzy wearing it back to the beach house.

While she was sitting there chuckling about Suzy, one of the puppies found Penny's top and started to drag it along the beach, Penny jumped up and grabbed it in the middle leaving a strap hanging free. The other pup decided he wanted to get in on the game and grabbed the strap, leaving Penny holding the bra with two pups pulling in opposite directions. The bra lost, and tore apart. The two pups took off, each with half a bra. Suzy bent over laughing.

"Serves you right, you thought it was funny when it was my top," said Suzy. Penny looked at her, sat down, and burst out laughing.

"Guess we have to learn how to live with two live wires," Suzy said.

Penny looked up. "We can still have a party to introduce the pups to our friends. How about Mars and Pax as names? War and Peace?"

Suzy grabbed the pup that was running with the destroyed bra. "This is Mars."

Penny picked up the pup sitting at her feet. "Then this is Pax."

Pax wore a red collar, and Mars's collar was blue. Right now, that was about the only distinguishing feature.

As the pups grew, Suzy would continue their training, and they would become great guard dogs. When Suzy whistled, they would come running and sit by her side, looking like two sentinels. They would never become vicious, but they looked like they would love to tear apart anyone who tried to harm Suzy. They would patrol the property, and no-one could just wander in unannounced.

* * *

The following weekend, when the pups were still small, Penny and Suzy invited the gang down to meet them. Suzy had set the sign to "TOPLESS – OPTIONAL." Suzy's option was always topless. She was there, with the dogs at her side, to welcome all. She wore her SCAD T-shirt and her yellow bikini bottom. It was obvious there was nothing but Suzy under the T-shirt. As they arrived, Suzy directed them to the beach. On the path to the beach, Suzy had erected a sign: "TIPEN BEACH IS NOT RESPONSIBLE FOR LOST OR DESTROYED ITEMS."

They all saw the sign, but paid little heed to it. David and Sam were the last to arrive. Suzy took them in the golf cart to the beach. When they passed the sign, David noticed it and asked, "Why?"

Suzy replied, "There have been some items missing and some vandalism. Nothing serious, just personal items."

Before David could question further, they reached the beach area and Suzy removed her T-shirt, and that took David's mind off the sign.

When they were all comfortable, with drinks in hand, Penny picked up a pup and announced, "This is Peace, Pax for short."

Suzy, picking up the other pup, said, "This is War, now known as Mars. Together they are the Terrible Two."

They put the two down and the dogs immediately started running around sniffing all the bags lying around. Their first find was MaryAnne's top, which Mars immediately grabbed, and he took off down the beach with Pax in close pursuit. Pax caught up and a tug-of-war began. By the time MaryAnne arrived, the top was shredded. There was much laughter and ladies scrambling to gather up anything loose.

Suzy laughed. "You all should have seen the sign. We're not liable. Besides, the pups have retained a good lawyer."

Penny got out a couple of tennis balls and threw them down the beach. The pups chased the balls and returned them to anyone wanting to play. They finally wore out and came to lie beside Suzy. The rest of the evening was peaceful. They built a fire and had hot dogs and beer, or wine for the more genteel. They talked until about 9 p.m., when it was time to leave.

Max stopped Penny to tell her that some of the men on her "list to be notified if arrested" had been picked up in a drug bust. These were the men who had provided Cavuto with an alibi. They were in jail and were being held until she had a chance to interview them—that is, all but one. Snake had managed to get bailed out. Penny went home full of hope and looked forward to tomorrow.

Chapter Nineteen

DUKE'S TRIAL PRELIMINARIES

T he next morning, Penny got up early, had her grapefruit juice, and took her usual run. She showered, dressed in a well-tailored suit, and headed for the jail. She would first interview Joe Martello. He had had only minor scrapes with the law, not enough to affect his sentence. She would have to take a different tack with him. She was seated in the interview room when they brought Joe in.

"Morning, Mr. Martello, please sit down. Would you like a cup of coffee? This may take some time."

Two cups were brought in.

Penny began, "Mr. Martello, the DA's office has notified the judge not to allow bail at this time."

Joe sputtered, "Why? Snake got out last night."

Penny fingered her paper and picked out a sheet. "Snake evidently has a friend with money, a good lawyer, and some influence. His lawyer was here before the cell was locked. Must be nice to know someone like that."

"I know him, not as well as Snake does, but he owes me a favor."

"Well, Snake did ask the lawyer about you and your friend, but he said only Snake, not the other two," replied Penny.

She let him think about that for a short time and said, "Mr. Martello, are you aware that you are involved in a murder case?"

Joe looked up. "Nah, I never did anything like murder, I just got busted for drugs."

"Five years ago, you helped provide an alibi for two men accused of murder. That's a serious offense."

"I don't remember nothing about that."

"You don't remember saying you were playing poker with Duke, Snake, and three others five years ago?"

"No, my memory ain't so good."

Penny replied, "Well, you'll probably be charged with obstruction of justice, accessory to murder, and a few minor charges. That could add up to twenty to life. Think about it. If you want to cooperate, we can probably get that reduced." She got up, packed her briefcase, and left. Joe was sitting there, staring at the wall.

Penny went to the station cafeteria and found Captain Feinstein sitting by himself. When he saw her, he stood and motioned for her to sit. After pleasantries, he asked her what brought her to the station. She told him about her session and that she was interviewing Kinky Roberts next. He had a long rap sheet and might be persuaded to see the light if it meant a lighter sentence. The captain said he might have some good news. He had located John Newton, one of the four poker players giving Duke an alibi.

"He is in a veteran's facility in Georgia. He is terminal and told his priest he wanted to clear up a mistake he made a few years ago, the lie about the poker game. I've schedule a trip for tomorrow. Want to come along and take a deposition?"

"You bet. Could be the beginning of the unraveling of the alibi. I will still talk to Kinky this afternoon and lay the groundwork for his conversion," said Penny.

* * *

Penny was waiting for Kinky when he was brought into the interview room. "Please sit down, Mr. Roberts."

"I want my lawyer present if you are gonna ask me questions, and why can't I get out on bail?" snapped Kinky.

Penny quietly answered. "You have that right and I won't ask you any questions this afternoon, but you are being held as a material witness in a murder case."

Mr. Roberts was taken aback. "What d'you mean, murder? I ain't been involved in no murder."

"Ah, maybe we'd better wait for your lawyer," answered Penny.

But Kinky was too excited to wait. "I want to know what you're talking about."

"OK, but remember, anything you say can be used against you."

"OK, OK, now tell me what this is all about."

"'Do you remember providing an alibi for Duke Cavuto by saying you and others were playing poker with him?"

"Yes, but that was to keep him from getting in trouble with his wife, not murder!" Roberts revealed.

"That's maybe what you were told, but at that time, Duke and Snake were committing a murder and they got you involved."

"We were told that Duke was with another woman and if his wife found out, she'd skin him alive. Duke was a person for whom you would like to do a favor, plus he gave us each fifty dollars."

The following day Penny and the captain went to Georgia and took a deposition from John Newton. As promised, he recanted his original story of playing poker with Duke and Snake. One step closer. John passed away that night.

Chapter Twenty

TRIAL BEGINS

On Monday, Max and Penny had a meeting with the DA and laid out their case. The DA's only question was, were they sure they could produce the original eyewitness? It had been almost five years. When they assured him they could, he told them to proceed. They contacted Captain Feinstein and mapped out the arrest of the two.

At 4 a.m. the next day, two officers knocked on Snake's door, and when the sleepy-eyed man opened the door and tried to shut it, they pushed it in and cuffed him.

"What the f…!"

"You are under arrest for the murder of Greg Anderson." They read him his rights and hauled him off to jail.

At the same time, Captain Feinstein, with two officers, knocked on the door of Duke's townhouse. It took some time before he opened the door. He had on a green silk robe and was definitely unhappy. He started to complain, "This had better be good."

The officers grabbed him and cuffed him. Captain Feinstein said, "Duke, I arrest you for the murder of Greg Anderson," and read him his rights.

Downtown, Duke and Snake only caught a glimpse of each other and were not able to communicate. Both had the feeling that they were in deep doo-doo. They were!

They were arraigned that afternoon, and the trial was set for the middle of the next month, in six weeks' time.

Penny and Max were ready. They had been waiting five years, but wanted to be sure there would be no mistakes, no misplaced commas or left out periods. They had a team of six lawyers, including themselves, and Captain Feinstein's crew. That crew would scrutinize the poker witnesses to be sure there were no surprises. They would also try to tie Duke to the two Russian thugs, which would definitely be icing on the cake.

The following month, they held meetings and discussed strategies, and Penny started writing her opening argument. She spent a great deal of time perfecting it and forcing both Suzy and Max to listen to it so much they would try to hide when they saw her coming with a piece of paper in her hand. Suzy would look out the window and see Penny standing on the beach, waving her arms and yelling at the surf. She tried to think. "Who was that guy that put marbles in his mouth to help him speak? Oh, well, Penny reminds me of him."

As the month passed, they were unable to find a connection between Duke and the Russians. Fortunately, it wasn't necessary. The fact that they were together and Timmy had heard Duke give them an order would be enough. She would tie it all together in her opening remarks.

* * *

The trial preliminaries were completed and everyone was seated.

"The prosecution may make her opening remarks," the judge said.

"Thank you, Your Honor," Penny began. "The prosecution shall prove beyond a shadow of a doubt that the defendants did willfully murder Greg Anderson and ordered the mutilation of Timothy Thomas and Jack Love, causing the death of Jack Love.

On the day noted, at approximately two-thirty p.m., Mr. Cavuto and Mr. Baer were heard entering Mr. Anderson's office on the eighth floor of Mr. Anderson's building. A witness will testify as to what transpired. The two defendants along with two Russian thugs entered the office. Mr. Anderson expressed in no uncertain terms that he was not interested in any conversation with the union organizer and ordered the group out.

"Cavuto took exception to Mr. Anderson's proclamation and ordered Baer to 'take him,' upon which Baer, from behind, hit Mr. Anderson with a blackjack, knocking him out.

"Cavuto then made the decision to drop Mr. Anderson down the drop chute, a fall of eight stories, resulting in his death. Cavuto then ordered the two Russian thugs to 'take care of those two' (Timothy and Jack) and send a message. Cavuto and Baer left, and the two thugs carried out their orders by mutilating both of the young men, killing Mr. Love. Both of the thugs were killed in a shootout with security police. All this, we will prove. Thank you, Your Honor."

"Does the defense wish to make an opening statement at this time?" asked the judge.

The defense replied, "No, Your Honor, not at this time."

"Then the prosecution may call its first witness."

"The prosecution calls Captain Feinstein." The captain took the stand and was sworn in.

Penny asked, "You were assigned to investigate the killings at the Anderson building?"

"Yes. We took the call and arrived after the security police had confronted the Russians. We found the two Russians dead, and one young man dead, and another young man wounded. An ambulance was called, for the wounded man, and we requested the coroner and a crime lab truck," said the captain.

"You didn't find Greg Anderson at that time?"

"No."

"When did you realize Mr. Anderson was missing?"

"The next day, when we interviewed Mr. Thomas, he asked about him. We returned to the building and found his body in the container at the bottom of the chute."

"That's all for this witness at this time, but reserve the right to recall," finished Penny.

The judge said, "Your witness, Mr. Defense Attorney."

"Thank you, Your Honor," the defense replied.

"Captain, did you at that time find anything that would tie the defendants into this crime?"

"Not at that time," replied the captain.

Before he had time to add anything, the defense attorney said, "No further questions."

"Your next witness, Ms. Prosecutor."

"I call Dr. Bowman, city coroner."

Dr. Bowman took the stand and was sworn in. Penny had the doctor give his name, his job, and his credentials.

She began, "Did you perform the autopsies on those murdered in this case?"

"My office did. I personally did Mr. Anderson and Mr. Love."

"Let's start with Mr. Anderson. What was the cause of death?"

"It was definitely the fall. He had multiple broken bones, internal injuries, and head injuries, any of which could have been the cause of death."

"Could you detect a blow to the head?"

"No, damage from the fall would mask that out."

"Could you determine if he was alive when he was put into the chute?"

"Yes, there is no doubt that he was alive when he hit the bottom."

"Now, let's go to Mr. Love. What was the cause of death?"

"Mr. Love died from asphyxiation. We found an article in his airway and he had tape over his mouth preventing him from ejecting it."

"Did you ascertain what that object was?"

"Yes, his penis had been cut off and forced down his throat," the coroner said. There were several gasps in the courtroom.

"And the two Russians?"

"Both had died from multiple gunshot wounds."

Penny said, "Your witness."

The defense asked, "Was there any forensic evidence that would tie anyone to the body before it was put into the chute?"

"No."

"No further questions."

The judge said to Penny, "Call your next witness."

Penny replied, "I call Captain Feinstein back to the stand. Tell us how the investigation progressed."

Captain Feinstein began, "We went to interview Mr. Thomas. He asked about Mr. Anderson. We were not aware that Mr. Anderson was involved. We had been trying to contact him, but had been unsuccessful. The investigation led us to the chute bin. When we went back to talk to Mr. Thomas, he told us the Duke and Snake were responsible for the murder of Mr. Anderson.

"We immediately began trying to establish their whereabouts during the time of the crime. We found four union members who swore they were playing poker with Snake and Duke during the time of the crime. The DA thought that the word of four union members was superior to that of one traumatized kid and decided not to prosecute. For over five years we kept the case open and only recently got a break."

"And what was that?" Penny asked.

Captain Feinstein continued, "Three of the poker players were arrested in a drug bust, giving us some leverage, and the other one decided he wanted to clear his conscience and gave a deathbed confession stating that he had lied because Duke asked him to and he received $50 for doing so. With the alibi destroyed and with the eyewitness, we felt the case was complete and ready for prosecution."

"No further questions, Your Honor."

The defense attorney began his questioning. "Captain Feinstein, do you believe we should now take the word of these drug dealers and liars?"

"I didn't take their words then, that's why we kept the case open. We just weren't able to break them. Circumstances changed and so did they."

"No further questions, Your Honor."

The judge pounded his gavel and announced, "The court will take a fifteen-minute break."

Chapter Twenty-One

TIMMY TESTIFIES

They had decided that Max would question Timmy. Penny would question the two poker players. They didn't believe Duke or Snake would take the stand. Penny left and Max returned to the courtroom. The judge called the court to order and told Max to call her next witness.

Max spoke to the judge. "Your Honor, the next witness is in the witness protection program and has requested his identity not be revealed. We have set up a screen and a microphone to disguise his voice. We have discussed all this with the defense."

"Is the defense satisfied with these arrangements?"

"Yes, as long as we are satisfied the witness is who he says he is."

"The prosecutor may continue," the judge said.

"We call Mr. Timothy Thomas to the stand." Timmy was sworn in.

"Before we go further, I call Dr. Samantha Webb to the stand." Dr. Sam was sworn in and took the stand.

Sam was sitting where she could be seen by the court and she could see behind the screen.

Max opened with, "Doctor, can you see the person behind the screen and do you know the individual?"

"Yes, I was his attending physician when he was wounded. He is Timothy Thomas."

"Thank you. I now call Agent David Webb." David was sworn in.

Max asked, "How are you acquainted with Mr. Thomas?"

David answered, "I was responsible for enrolling him in the witness protection program. At present, I am his only contact with the bureau."

"Is this Timothy Thomas, and is he the individual who was the witness to the murder of Greg Anderson and Jack Love?"

"Yes."

"Your witness."

Defense started, "When was the last time you saw him?"

David replied, "That would be the day before yesterday when he came to see me about the trial."

"Then you are sure this is Timothy Thomas."

"Yes."

"No further questions."

The judge turned and said to Max, "You may proceed with this witness."

Max began. "Please state your name."

"Timothy Thomas."

"Where were you on November sixteenth?"

"I was working at the Anderson building."

"Tell us what happened on that day."

"Jack and I were working on an A/C installation, around two," said Timmy. "We heard a group come into the boss's office. The conversation started at a reasonable level, but soon the voices got loud and angry."

"Were you able to understand what was said?"

"Yes, the walls were just made of single sheets of plywood. You could hear normal conversation clearly and they were talking loudly, eventually yelling."

"What did you hear?"

"First we heard some conversation to which we didn't pay attention, but when we heard Greg raise his voice, we started to listen."

"What did he say?"

"He said, 'Certainly I know who you are, you're Duke the union sleaze. I'm not interested in any discussion with you or any union guy.' He sounded very angry, and Jack and I started for the door to Greg's office. I heard Duke say, 'Well, Mister high and mighty, what if your next building is delayed because the contractors you hire have union problems? Work with me and I can see there will be no problems and in the end we'll both make money.'

"At this time, it was apparent the boss was very mad when he yelled, 'Take your hooligans and get your ass out of my building.' When Jack and I were going through the door, we heard Duke shout, 'No shit talks to me that way, take him, Snake.' I saw Snake hit the boss with what I thought was a blackjack. I saw the boss fall."

"Then what happened?" Max asked

"As Jack and I raced through the door, Jack was in front, and someone stepped behind Jack and hit him. He went down hard. As I passed through the door, I was hit. I went down, but was not unconscious. There were two thugs just inside, they grabbed me and tied my arms to the legs of the desk. They taped my mouth. I heard Duke say, 'Let's drop him down the chute.' I saw Duke and Snake carrying Greg toward the chute. I couldn't see them drop him in the chute, but I heard something falling," explained Timmy.

"Did you see Duke and Snake again?"

"Only once when they came over to tell the two thugs, 'Take care of those two and be sure to send a message.' The two answered, 'Sure thing, boss.'"

"What did Duke do then?"

"I couldn't see them, but I heard them leave, taking the stairs," said Timmy.

"What happened next?"

"The two thugs went to Jack, cut off his penis, and put it in his mouth. Then they put a piece of tape over his mouth. He struggled to get to the tape on his mouth but his hands were restrained. I watched him struggle until the two came to me. My legs were free and I rolled and kicked, trying my best to prevent them from restraining me. They finally did restrain me. While they were doing Duke's bidding, I passed out."

"What's the next thing you remember?"

"I thought I heard shots. The next thing I remember, I was in the hospital being cared for by a beautiful nurse, except she wasn't a nurse, she was a doctor, Dr. Samantha Webb. She specialized in reconstructive surgery."

"Thank you for your testimony, I'm sure it was very unpleasant to relive your experience." Turning to the defense, Max said, "Your witness."

The defense counsel said to the judge, "I wish to state that having to question this witness under these circumstances is detrimental to my client's case and I would like to protest. It's been five years and my client is in jail, what harm can he do to this witness?"

Max jumped to her feet and said, "I object, Your Honor, the defense has agreed to this and is trying to influence the jury with this statement. If I may, Your Honor, I will explain the reason for protecting his identity."

The judge said, "Please do."

"After the crime, it was decided that the witness was in grave danger and was put into the witness protection program. He gave up his past. He was an architect, but because it was decided that it would be dangerous to pursue a job in that field, he went into an entirely different field and started a new life with new friends and associates. He feels he doesn't want to disrupt that life at this time."

"Objection denied, the defense will continue."

The defense stood up and continued, "If you only saw Duke and Snake this one time, how can you be sure of their identity?"

"After I told the lieutenant that Duke and Snake did it, they had a pictorial lineup. I was shown a bunch of pictures, and I had no trouble picking them out. I had every reason to remember them," said Timmy.

"You didn't actually see them drop Mr. Anderson down the chute?"

"No, as I said, I was tied to the desk and was on the floor. My view was limited, I could only see part of the office."

"Then you can't swear it was Mr. Cavuto and Mr. Baer who dropped Mr. Anderson down the chute?"

Without hesitation, Timmy answered, "No."

"Thank you, that's all."

"Do you have any redirect?"

Max answered, "Yes. Mr. Thomas, although you couldn't see the chute, could you hear what was happening?"

"Yes, I could hear everything. I saw them carry Mr. Anderson, and when I couldn't see them, I heard them continue over to the chute, and I heard a heavy object drop down the chute. I heard Mr. Cavuto tell the Russians 'Take care of them and send a message.'"

Max continued, "Then what happened?"

"I heard Cavuto and his associate, Snake, go down the stairs. The two Russians mutilated and killed Jack. I heard the elevator moving. It was then I fought with the Russian and it was during that time I passed out."

"Thank you. That's all, Your Honor."

"Does the defense have any further questions?"

The defense replied, "No, Your Honor."

"This witness is excused. The court will take a fifteen-minute recess.

During the recess, Penny rejoined Max and they discussed how the trial had gone so far. Both were satisfied.

Chapter Twenty-Two

TRIAL CONTINUES

The judge called the court to order and told Penny to call her next witness.

"The prosecution would like to read a deposition from Mr. John Newton, who passed away recently. He gave this on his deathbed."

The judge turned to Penny and asked, "Does the defense have a copy of the deposition?"

"Yes, Your Honor."

"You may proceed."

Penny started to read. "This document was dated the seventh of last month, at the Veterans' Facility in Augusta, Georgia. It reads: I, John Newton swear the following is a true and accurate account of the happening five years ago when I swore I was playing poker with Duke Cavuto, Snake Baer, and three others on the afternoon of the murder of Greg Anderson. We were told Duke was with a woman, not his wife, and if his wife found out, there would be hell to pay. Any union member would be happy to do Duke a favor, plus he gave us each fifty dollars. It was not true that Duke and Snake played cards with us the whole time. We started the game at noon. Duke and Snake didn't get there until after five-thirty p.m. They played a couple of hands and we broke up."

Penny concluded, "This statement was witnessed by myself, Captain Feinstein, and Father Fitzgerald. I submit a copy of the deposition to the court as Exhibit 4b."

The judge looked at the defense attorney, who said, "No objection."

The judge told Penny, "Call your next witness."

Penny said, "The defense calls Mr. Joe Martello."

Joe took the stand and was sworn in.

"Mr. Martello, where are you living right now?"

Joe looking a little confused. "Right now at the city jail. Why? I was picked up in a drug bust."

"Did you testify five years ago that you and three others were playing poker all afternoon with Mr. Cavuto and a man known as Snake?"

"Yes, we were asked to say that to help Duke out. He told us he was with another woman and his wife would skin him alive if she found out."

"Why did you agree?"

"Doing Duke a favor might mean a favor in return. He has lots of influence in the union, and he gave us fifty dollars each."

"Was Mr. Cavuto there for the whole game?"

"No. He and Snake came in around five-thirty, played a couple of hands, and left."

"Did Duke ever repay the favor?" queried Penny.

"Sure, I got a number of jobs because Duke recommended me. He would stop and tell me about a job and say, 'I still owe you, old buddy.'"

"What did you think that meant?"

"That he would continue to get me jobs."

"And what did you have to do?"

"Never thought about it."

"Why did you decide to come clean now?"

"Well, when Winky confessed, I figured it would better for me to make a clean break of it. I honestly wasn't aware of the murder."

"That's all. Your witness," Penny concluded.

The defense attorney responded, "No questions."

Penny turned to the judge and said, "The prosecution rests."

The judge asked, "Is the defense ready?"

The defense attorney rose and requested a recess until the following day.

"Does the prosecutor have any objection?" asked the judge.

"No objection, Your Honor."

"The court will recess until tomorrow at ten a.m."

Chapter Twenty-Three

BEACH BREAK

Penny decided the gang needed a break from the trial and suggested they all go down to the beach for the evening. The pups were there to greet them, full of vim and vigor. Suzy had prepared steaks, baked potatoes, and a salad.

During dinner, Suzy told them about the dogs and some intruders. One day when Penny was there for lunch, two scruffy looking young men had wandered onto the property and decided to make themselves at home. The two pups made the intruders' presence known by incessant barking. When Penny and Suzy went outside, the two men and the two dogs were standing face to face. Suzy whistled and the two dogs ran and sat by her side.

Suzy looked at the men and told them, "This is private property, I'd appreciate your leaving immediately."

The bigger of the two answered in a low Cracker voice, "We kinda like it here," and, looking at Penny and Suzy in their bikinis with a lustful stare, added, "We like what we see."

Suzy, in a disgusted voice, gave an icy reply. "Kiddies, in less than five minutes, there will be a sheriff car here, complete with two deputies. If you get your asses in gear, you can be gone by then. If not you'll be arrested for trespassing. Your choice."

The two looked at each other and smiled, and the smaller one said, "I think we ought to at least have a taste of southern hospitality before we leave." He started toward Suzy. The other one reached for Penny. Instantly, Mars leaped into action, getting between the man and Suzy. Penny moved quickly as the man attempted to grab her, and soon had him on his back with her foot on his neck. Pax was standing over him with his teeth bared when the sheriff's car arrived.

The two men decided the game was up and they had lost. "Looks as if you have things well in hand," quipped the deputy. "What's your pleasure?"

Penny sighed. "Just show them off the property. I don't think they'll return. Fellows, tell your friends this property is off limits. The next ones won't be treated so nicely."

The deputies walked the two men to their car. The dogs followed them to the gate and then ran back to Suzy. Suzy told Penny she was considering putting in a security gate, although, with the terrible two, she didn't think it would be needed.

Chapter Twenty-Four

TRIAL CONCLUDES

The judge called the court to order. "Does the defense wish to present an opening remark?"

"Your Honor, the defense rests."

The judge asked Penny, "Is the prosecution ready for her closing statement?"

Penny answered, "Yes, Your Honor," and moved in front of the jury.

She began. "The prosecution has provided indisputable evidence that Mr. Cavuto and Mr. Baer did cause the death of Mr. Greg Anderson and Mr. Jack Love. They fabricated an alibi by bribing four men who have since recanted their stories. Mr. Thomas was an eyewitness to the event and gave a detailed description of the murders of Greg Anderson and Jack Love along with the mutilation of two young men. The evidence is there, and I'm sure you will come back with a verdict of murder in the first degree. Thank you for your attention."

The judge asked, 'Is the defense ready?"

"Yes, Your Honor," replied the defense council. "The prosecution has laid out a convincing case, using the memory of a traumatized young man, of something that happened five years ago, and the testimony of five drug dealers. Seems pretty slim to convict two men of murder. Two Russian thugs were found at the crime scene and died in a gun battle. Isn't it more plausible that these two committed the murders? And that Mr. Cavuto was really with a woman, not his wife? When you discuss the evidence, think about the terrible things the two thugs did to those two young men, and think, if you were one of them, how clear would you be thinking? And the drug men, even though they said Mr. Cavuto came to the poker game late, all said they thought he was with another woman. Before you decide, remember, 'beyond a shadow of a doubt.' Consider carefully and you will find my client 'not guilty.' Thank for you attention."

The defense attorney sat down and the judge asked Penny, "Do you have a rebuttal?"

Penny replied, "Yes, Your Honor."

"Ladies and gentlemen of the jury, it is the defense attorney's job, nay, his duty to present an alternative to the prosecution's case. The defense did a creditable job, except there are holes that needed to be filled. First and prime is motive. Why would these two Russian thugs take an elevator up eight floors to rob three men who probably had less money than they could have got by robbing a convenience store, with much less risk? Why mutilate the two young men? Yes, this young man went through a terrible ordeal, but he was very alert the next day when he was interrogated. We were never introduced to the 'woman, not his wife.' The one that Mr. Cavuto was supposed to have been with during the time of the murder. Consider, as I know you will, all the evidence, and you will return a verdict of guilty of murder in the first degree. Thank you for your attention."

The judge gave his instructions to the jury. They retired to deliberate.

The jury was out for only five and a half hours. Penny and Max rushed back to the courtroom to hear the verdict. They had been seated for about ten minutes when the court was called to order. When the judge and the jury were all in and seated, the judge uttered the familiar "Have you reached a verdict?"

The jury foreman replied, "We have, Your Honor.

"We find the defendants guilty of the murder of Greg Anderson and Jack Love."

Penny sighed in relief. Five years of waiting had come to fruition. She hugged Max as they listened to the remaining courtroom formalities. A date was set for the sentencing, and the court was adjourned. After talking with other members of their team and receiving congratulations from many people, Penny and Max were able to get free. They headed to Penny's condo for a small celebration, which turned out to be not really small.

By the time they reached the condo, many of Penny's friends had already arrived for the victory party. Suzy had set up a bar and prepared food for a small army. They all wanted to congratulate Penny and Max. Suzy got out the champagne and filled glasses for all and proposed a toast, "To Penny and Max, to justice fulfilled, and to more time at the beach."

They all raised their glasses and laughed. There was the usual level of chatter of a cocktail party as they discussed the trial and the verdict. It was at this time that Penny announced Max was going to challenge the DA in the next election and she was resigning from the DA's office to work on her campaign. There were many questions and comments and offers to help. The party ended after midnight. It was a tired and happy group that left the condo.

Penny and Suzy slept late, and for once, Penny skipped her morning run. She showed up at the office and submitted her resignation to Max. They decided they would keep it at a low level so as few as possible were aware of it. It would be effective immediately, but it would make its way slowly through the bureaucracy. She cleaned out her desk and quietly left.

Chapter Twenty-Five

FAREWELL/HELLO

Penny called Dr. Sam, David, Dr. MaryAnne, Max, Kathy, Harriet, and Ellie, inviting them to a farewell party. She wouldn't tell them anything more. They all arrived at Penny's beach house on the Friday following the sentencing of Duke Cavuto.

Suzy had various tidbits on the tables and handed each guest a martini as they arrived. She told them to grab a seat, and then she let them chat until they had finished their drinks and they all seemed comfortable. She then passed around glasses of champagne and told them Penny wanted to make a toast.

Standing up, Penny toasted, "Farewell to Timmy." They all held up their glasses and drank their champagne. Max, Harriet, and Ellie drank, but had quizzical looks on their faces.

Penny said, "I'll start this, and the appropriate people will pick it up when they are involved. First, I apologize to Max, Harriet, and Ellie. I have kept you in the dark since I first met you.

"As we go through this, I hope you will understand that I thought it was for your own and my protection. We just toasted Timmy, and I think you all know that Timmy was the witness who put Cavuto away. What you didn't know is that I am—or I was—Timmy."

The looks on Max's, Harriet's, and Ellie's faces were indescribable.

Penny continued her explanation. "If you remember, I left the courtroom before Timmy testified. Sam was in a secure room on the third floor of the court. She helped me put on a disguise, and I went to the door that led to the area behind the security screen. When I finished, I went back to the room, removed the disguise, and returned through the front door and took my seat at the table.

"Let's go back to the birth of Penny. It started in the hospital when Sam was caring for me. We talked a lot about finding a way to keep me safe from Cavuto.

"Lieutenant Feinstein, David, and I discussed my getting a new identity and going out west. David acquired all the necessary papers, and everyone assumed that's what I did. In the meantime, I kept talking with Sam and told her I really didn't want to leave. I wanted to stay and see that Cavuto received his just due.

"During our discussion, Sam looked at me, and said she thought there was a way, but it was drastic. I told her I was listening. She told me that since I was a small person and I already had long hair and fair skin with little body hair, she could give me a face so I could pass as a female. She let me think about it overnight. What people didn't know was that when the paper reported that she put me back together they assumed she reattached my penis.

"Dr. Sam, it's your turn," Penny concluded.

Dr. Sam took up the narrative. "The damage was too great for me to reattach the penis, and all I could do was perform surgery that allowed him to carry out his normal body function as we girls do. He has to sit when he goes. I also decided to move his testicles up into a body cavity and sewed them in. None of this information was ever released.

"When the surgery had healed, he could put on a bikini and it would be difficult to know he was a male. As we talked, and he kept talking about not really wanting to leave the area, I told him of the possibility of posing as a female. It was a very difficult decision, but his desire to stay was the deciding factor. David got all new papers giving life to Penelope O'Dowd. No one knew except David and myself.

"We took 'Penny' home to live in the apartment over our garage. 'Her' wardrobe for the first week was two dainty nighties and a floral print housecoat. By the end of the week it became apparent that the DA was not going to aggressively pursue Cavuto, and Penny may have to exist for some time. 'Penny' decided to go through with the facial surgery to give her a feminine look. As you can see, I gave her a very perky button nose, puffed up her cheeks, and did a little tuck here and a little tuck there.

"By the end of a year, Penny was in law school and we had a talk about being Penny or being Timmy. She discussed what it would be like to return to Timmy. Her thoughts were that she could no more be a man than she was a woman. She could continue to build a life as Penny, but it would be very difficult to continue that life as Timmy.

"It was then we started discussing hormone treatments. I told her that treatment was not reversible, that she would develop breasts and might put some fat on her hips and buttocks. She would not turn into a female but she would look more like a woman. She said she had no desire to be a female. She decided she wanted to talk to her sister Kathy before she started any treatment."

David stood up and continued the story. "Kathy had finished her studies in France and was back in New England finishing her work on her doctorate degree. Kathy knew Timmy was in some kind of witness protection program but had no idea where he was, or what name he was using. Kathy understood that this was for her protection as well as his.

"When I contacted her, I explained that Timmy wanted to see her but it had to done in secret. She was to develop a logical reason for coming to Florida, maybe even a vacation with a friend.

"After arriving in Miami, she was to make an appointment with Dr. MaryAnne Taylor, who would give her instructions on meeting Timmy. I mentioned the need of secrecy and this was not to be discussed with anyone else. She acknowledged this and said she would try to be there by the following weekend. I gave her my private cell phone number and told her to use it as a last resort. We said good-bye and I told her I would see her when she got here."

It was Kathy's turn to continue the narrative.

"I was surprised and disturbed by David's call. Many nights I had gone to bed wondering where Timmy was and what he was doing and hoping it wouldn't be long before I could at least see him. It looked as if the time had come. I had no problem creating a reason to visit Florida. I was still doing research on my thesis and I could actually use a couple of days at the UM library. I made my roommates and the faculty aware of my plans. I arranged for flights and for lodging at a motel near the university. I would leave early Friday morning and be in Miami by noon.

"As soon as I was checked in at my motel and got settled, I called Dr. MaryAnne's office and asked to speak to the doctor. She answered and I told her my name and that I wanted an appointment. She said her last appointment was at four-thirty, and if I could be there, she could work me in. I was there right on time. The way I looked, I was sure the staff thought I must have a real medical problem. The staff was buttoning up, getting ready to go home. The previous patient came to the checkout desk and I heard the doctor tell the staff they could go home, she could handle the last patient herself.

"When they had left, the doctor came to the door and asked me to follow her. She took me to an examining room and had me sit while she proceeded to examine me. I started to protest when she whispered that there was one staff member left. She had to have some records of my visit, so she asked me to relax and have a free examination.

"By the time she had finished taking my blood pressure and checking my heart and lungs, the final staff member had left. Dr. MaryAnne finished making notes and handed me a prescription. She indicated for me to follow her to her office. It was small but comfortable. She sat at her desk and I took a soft, overstuffed leather chair. I sat there looking at the prescription. She had written me a prescription for birth control pills. She explained, why else would a healthy young lady make a rush appointment with a doctor? She suggested I have it filled at a pharmacy near the university.

"Dr. MaryAnne said she was not sure if all this secrecy was necessary, but didn't want to take chances with people's lives, especially people she loves. It would all be made clear later. I was to go to room five-oh-six at the Hotel Intercontinental downtown at seven p.m. She said there would be food and drinks, so not to worry about having dinner. She told me she'd be there and would open the door when I knocked, so I'd know it was all right. She stood up and gave me a hug and showed me the way out.

"I had a little time to kill and went to a Walgreens pharmacy near the university and had my prescription filled. I headed downtown to the hotel and arrived a little early. I wanted a drink, something hard, or at least a coffee. I decided against it. Coffee would only increase my nervousness and I didn't want the smell of alcohol on my breath. I spent ten minutes in a news shop at the hotel and finally bought a magazine. I didn't even know which one I bought. I could wait no longer and headed to the elevator to go to the fifth floor. I knocked on the door and Dr. MaryAnne opened it. She had a big smile on her face and indicated for me to come on in.

I entered and there were two other women and a man. MaryAnne introduced them: first David Webb, with whom I had talked, his wife, Dr. Sam, and a young lady she introduced as Penny. We all sat down and MaryAnne passed around martinis, saying, 'Take this, you may need it.' I took it, took a healthy drink, and asked where Timmy was.

"The young lady, Penny, walked over to me and said in a familiar voice, 'Kathy, I'm Timmy.' Stunned, flabbergasted, bewildered, I could find no words to express my feeling. I stood up, looking at her face. I could see Timmy. Simultaneously we reached for each other and hugged. I knew we both had tears in our eyes and through moist eyes I saw the other three with big smiles on their faces.

"Timmy/Penny and I continued to hold each other and moved to a couch where we sat and held each other. Penny continued explaining that only the people in that room knew who she was. She explained that Dr. Sam was the surgeon who took care of him after the mutilation and did the work on his face. David, Dr. Sam's husband, was an FBI agent and was responsible for arranging all the papers and Timmy's exit from the hospital. He was the only contact between the authorities and Timmy.

"Dr. MaryAnne had become Penny's family physician as they wanted to separate Penny from Dr. Sam professionally and they felt they needed a trustworthy doctor to take care of her. MaryAnne was a longtime friend of Sam. They had attended med school together and it was not surprising that they would be friends socially. It was through this relationship that Penny became friends with MaryAnne and, through her, developed a social friendship with Sam. They had become best friends.

I noted that they all referred to Timmy as 'Penny' and used the feminine gender. That was something I would have to work on: having a girl friend, not a brother.

"Penny explained to me that the reason they got me here was twofold. First, they didn't think Cavuto was actively looking for Timmy anymore. As long as he was convinced Timmy was still out west and in hiding, he would just wait, so the danger was not great.

"Second, she stated that since posing as a female for over a year she had begun to build a future. She didn't know if she could continue her career if she became Timmy again. She had become completely comfortable being a female, and even if she did revert to Timmy, she would be no more a man than she is a female.

"She decided to stay as a female but wanted to know if I had any problem with it. I told her, I lost a brother and gained a new best girlfriend. Actually, we can do a lot more as girlfriends then we could as brother and sister and probably argue less. I said, if that's what you want, I'm all for it."

She reached over and gave Penny a hug.

Dr. MaryAnne said, "So Penny decided to start hormone treatments. As we told her, the treatments were irreversible. She would develop breasts and might fill out in other parts of the body. She would not become a female but would take on a more feminine appearance.

"She came in every month for a checkup and a treatment. It took about two years for the treatments to have full effects. She has done beautifully.

Sam and I also gave her instructions in living as a lady. We took her on shopping tours, telling her what to buy and how to wear it. While she still was living over Sam's garage, we had her buy a pair of heels. This took a Herculean effort at first, to get her to try walking in them and then to practice walking. For someone as athletic as she is and who runs two miles a day, we had a blast watching her trying to go five steps without breaking stride. We were most sympathetic, offering words of encouragement when we could quit laughing."

"Yes, they were sympathetic," interjected Penny. "They sat on the bed as I tried to walk and made some very derogatory remarks like, 'Looks like a duck trying to walk on stilts' or 'Bet you a buck she can't make five without breaking stride' and 'Five to one, and I'll take that bet," and they would fall back on the bed choking in laughter. So I stopped and said I'd try again tomorrow.

'We'll be here,' they said as they left. When they'd left, I put the shoes on and practiced. I worked all evening. By bedtime, I was able to not only walk but run, and walk up and down stairs without stumbling. They arrived early the next day. It was Sunday and with big grins on their faces they said they came to take me to church in my new high heels, but I should practice so I wouldn't embarrass them. They sat on the bed awaiting the show. I went to the chair across the room to put on my shoes. They started, 'I'll give twenty to one she won't make five steps without breaking stride' and 'I'll do better, I'll give twenty-five to one!' Still in my stocking feet I walked over to the bed and gave each one of them a five dollar bill and said, 'You're on.' I put on the shoes, stood up, and with the air of a model, walked over to the bed and said, 'That was seven steps, you two owe me two hundred and twenty-five dollars,' and I turned and walked back across the room, and said, 'I'll now get ready to go to church.' 'We've been had, I heard Sam whisper to MaryAnne. It was a stage whisper so I could hear her.

"Several times I almost decided to chuck it all and really go out west. But they wouldn't let me quit. I couldn't have done it without their help, even though they wouldn't cut me any slack. The first time we went to the mall, Sam made sure we stopped in every restroom in the mall so I would be sure to know which I should use. She even went so far as to put a 'ladies' room' sign on the bathroom in my apartment. They were always there to give me encouragement when I needed it. They even took me to Paris with them, but I thought of myself as a pet as much as a traveling companion.

"Another toast," said Sam. "Hello to Penny."

Max, Harriet, and Ellie had been engrossed with what they heard. Ellie said she could not believe that neither of them had ever had an inkling of Penny's deception, but they realized the reason for it. They both gave Penny a hug, and then Penny gave all the others a hug, and when she got to David, she not only gave him a hug but a big kiss.

"Gee, Penny, I told you not to do that when Sam was around. You know how jealous she is," he said in a loud whisper, which got him a slap on the back.

Penny went over to Max and Ellie and gave them each a dollar. "I just gave you a retainer for your professional service, so if anyone asks you, you can honestly say you cannot divulge anything you heard tonight because of lawyer/client confidentiality." They both smiled.

Penny proclaimed, "What started out to be secret among three is now among eight. I hope that's as many as ever need to know. You may have questions which you hesitate to ask, but go ahead, now is the time. I don't want you to be sitting across the room from me wondering about if I put my panty hose on correctly or did I shave my underarms, etcetera. So ask."

Ellie asked, "What was most difficult?"

She explained, "Remembering to answer to 'Penny' would have been, if Sam hadn't kept using it every time possible during that first six weeks and sharply reproaching me when I didn't answer quickly. Of course, she would quickly turn on a smile to be sure I knew it was because she cared.

"And even with wearing high heels, putting on panty hose, buttoning a bra behind my back, and being ladylike in a skirt, the most difficult thing for me was carrying a purse, a measurable difference between a man and a woman. The first skirt Sam got me was a denim one with pockets. I filled the pockets with everything I carried as a man. I thought Sam was going to choke when she saw me. She immediately got one of her old purses, one with a shoulder strap, and had me empty my pockets into it. From then on, I wasn't allowed to have pockets. She put a sign on the inside of my front door that said 'Your purse : don't leave home without it.' Sam thought for a while she was going to have to handcuff my purse to my wrist. It took a long time for it to become second nature to carry a purse."

Chapter Twenty-Six

DA ATTACK

Penny then broke the news that she had resigned from her job as a prosecutor effective immediately. Of course, Max knew this as she was the one who had received Penny's notice. There were questions about why she had done it.

When everyone had sat down, Suzy asked if anyone cared for anything, and she filled a couple of requests for drinks.

Penny explained that she was going to begin campaigning for Max, who had finally decided to run for the position of district attorney. Penny went on to explain that now Cavuto had been convicted, she had set her sights on the current DA, who she thought was both crooked and incompetent. She felt he should have taken a more aggressive action against Cavuto when he committed the murder of Greg and Jack. Helping Max get elected would be the best way she could see to get rid of the DA.

Ellie asked if they knew that the DA was going to personally prosecute a guy in the treasury office for embezzlement. They asked how she knew since they had not heard anything about it.

She said the man charged had come into her office inquiring about an attorney. She had explained that they didn't have a criminal defense attorney available. He said he guessed he would have to accept a public defender, as he couldn't afford the prices of the attorneys he had contacted.

Penny asked Ellie what she thought of the man.

"He seemed like a nice man in trouble, over his head," Ellie said, "and if I was to make a snap judgment, I think he's probably innocent."

"Why would the DA decide to prosecute this case himself?"

"Haven't you heard? The DA is on a 'clean up corruption in government' kick. It's part of his reelection campaign," said Ellie.

Penny responded, "I hadn't heard about it, I've been tied up lately. I resigned my position last week. Only Max knows, and she's processing it through the department on a slow boat. I'm going to devote my time to helping Max get elected as DA. He is the only one left who I feel was responsible for the failure to prosecute Duke. I'm going to do my damnedest to see him leave office."

"How can I help?" offered Ellie.

"Could you use a criminal lawyer on your staff? One that works cheap."

Ellie look surprised. "Do you really want to?"

"Yes, and do you think you can contact that man and tell him that if he wants, you found him a lawyer, real cheap, like pro bono?" said Penny.

"Sure thing, I believe I can have him available sometime tomorrow."

"Fine, let me know when."

Ellie grinned. "I can't wait to tell the mother hen that her favorite gofer is coming back."

They both laughed. Ellie smiled and said, "Maybe I should reconsider. I had this part-time help once and I was never able to control her. When do you want to start?"

"Tomorrow!"

* * *

The next day, Penny showed up at Ellie's law office, ready to do business. They gave her a desk and access to the conference room. As the partners came in and found that Penny had returned and would be working out of their office, they all stopped by to welcome her back.

Mother hen was especially happy to have her back, and kiddingly said, "I've got a whole list of things to be done."

Penny laughed and gave her a big hug. "It's good to be back."

Mr. Appleby had a 10 a.m. appointment, and Penny spent the remaining time checking on him. She Googled "George Appleby" which came back: treasurer, Long Palm, Florida; elected and reelected three times; degree from the University of Miami—and no other information. She went to the sheriff's system and found that in the last twenty years, he had gotten one parking ticket. He was an assistant scoutmaster and had coached Little League—a typical hardened criminal.

"Why would they pick him to use as an example?" thought Penny.

When Mr. Appleby came in, he and Penny went into the conference room. "Please be seated" Penny said. "And would you like something to drink?"

"No, thank you," he replied.

"Mr. Appleby, would you like me as your attorney?"

"Oh, yes, I appreciate your offer!"

Picking up a legal pad, Penny said, "OK, now, Mr. Appleby, tell me the whole story. Take your time. Do you mind if I record what you have to say?"

"No, but I'm not sure where to begin."

"When were you first notified of the shortage?"

Mr. Appleby began. "Well, my wife and I took a three-week cruise. It was our twenty-fifth anniversary. When we got back and I went to the office, the door was locked and I was told to report to the mayor. People were looking at me in a peculiar manner, I didn't know why. When I got to his office, I knocked and went in. No greeting, no 'How was your trip,' just 'Sit down, George, we have a problem.'"

Mr. Appleby went on to describe his conversation with the mayor. "The mayor informed me that there is a considerable shortage in my books and asked for an explanation. I told him I had no idea what he was talking about and would have to examine the books first.

At that point he said that the DA told them not to let me get near the books and that a professional had recently audited them. He told me I had a week to find an attorney and that I was to be in court the next Tuesday."

Mr. Appleby turned to Penny. "I was dumbfounded. I didn't know what to say. I went home and told my wife. We just sat there with the TV on, not saying anything. I told her I had no idea what it was all about. There were no problems when I left. She hugged me and said not to worry, we would get a lawyer and fight it. That made me feel better, but I thought, what are we fighting? I still don't know where or how the money is missing."

"George, come Monday—or before—we will have all that information! One dumb question: Do you know anything about any discrepancies in your books?" queried Penny.

George answered, "No. There is a peculiarity in the books that has been there for a number of years. Everyone concerned knows about it and a competent auditor would find it and not report it as a problem. I had just done a thorough check before we left. Everything was fine."

Penny pondered, "Do you know anyone who would want to alter the books for any reason?"

"No, I don't know what anyone could gain. Of course, I don't know exactly where the discrepancy is," responded George.

Penny told George not to worry. She would get a copy of the indictment and they would work it out.

After George left, Penny found Ellie and told her they needed to talk when she had some free time. "How about lunch at Bill's, it should be quiet at one-thirty."

Penny replied, "Sounds good. I'll meet you there."

When they were seated and had ordered, Penny started, "I'm going to need an assistant. Someone not well known to the DA's office."

"How much experience does the person need?"

"I need a lawyer willing to put in lots of hours at low pay. He or she doesn't need experience. That will come from working in the courtroom."

"Then you would consider a recent grad?"

"Got someone in mind?" Penny quizzed.

Ellie said, "I just interviewed a recent grad, a young man that I think has lots of potential. His area of interest is criminal law and he's eager to learn. I think he would jump at the chance to work with you."

"He sounds good. Can you give me his phone number and I can set up an interview? I hate taking up your time with my problems, but I think I will need an office and a secretary. Is the office next to you still empty"?

Ellie nodded. Penny said, "Good, I'll see about leasing it and hiring a secretary. We will be under your company, business wise, but I will be responsible for all personnel and expenses. Is that OK with you?"

Ellie answered, "Yes, and I don't think we need to do anything formal right now. Just remember, I know a good lawyer." They both smiled, got up, and hugged.

That afternoon, Penny did lease the office. She also made an appointment with James Custard Jr. for the next day and called an agency about a secretary. The day was still early, so she drove to the beach house to visit Suzy for the evening.

When she drove through the gate, she saw the "Dress at Tipen Beach" sign Suzy had erected. It had a replaceable slat with a word painted in yellow, "Optional!"

She smiled, thinking of the first day when Suzy had declared the beach "topless." Suzy was waiting for her, wearing a yellow bikini. She ran up, gave Penny a hug and a kiss, and handed her a glass of cold wine. Penny took a swallow and rushed inside to don a bathing suit. Suzy had packed snacks and cold drinks.

They put everything in the golf cart and headed for the beach. When they got there, Suzy ripped off her top and yelled, "It's optional and I opt for topless!" Penny immediately followed, shedding her top. They spent the rest of the day enjoying each other's company, frolicking in the surf and taking the sun. They did not talk about the upcoming trial. When the sun finally set, providing another gorgeous pink and blue sky, they packed up and went back to the beach house. It was too hot for a fire so they opened the drapes and watched the surf roll in.

They were on the couch, Suzy lying on her back with her head in Penny's lap. Neither had spoken for some time, when Suzy said, "So how are things going?" Penny filled her in on what had happened in the past couple of days. She told Suzy she had to be back early the next day and she might be tied up the rest of the week. They went to bed early and slept cuddled up. They were up early the next morning.

While Penny showered, dressed, and put on her makeup, Suzy prepared breakfast: grapefruit juice, soft boiled eggs, crisp bacon, English muffins, and orange marmalade. When they finished breakfast, Penny got into her car, and after a long kiss through the car window, left for the drive home. She used the time on the drive back to think through the case. Why did they decide to charge

George, and why now? Was there more involved than the missing funds? Was it possible that they made a hasty decision to have a trial at this time and without adequate preparation? First, she must find out about the theft George was accused of.

Penny met with James Custard Jr. at her new office, and she was impressed with his poise and knowledge.

She explained that he would be her assistant and do things she wouldn't have time to do. She also explained that she didn't want the DA to know of her involvement until the trial, and therefore James would be the interface between her office and the DA's office.

"All contacts will be through you, and you will be with me during the trial," said Penny. "Your job during the trial will be to see that I am up to date on all matters pertaining to the trial. I want you to watch and listen and tell me about anything of interest you see or hear. Are you OK with that? What are you called? I can't keep calling you Mr. Custard."

Smiling, he responded, "My family calls me James. My friends call me Jimmy."

Penny said, "Your choice."

"Let's make it Jimmy."

Penny looked up and said, "OK, Jimmy, isn't that the name of superman's friend? Your first task is to go to the DA's office and get whatever you can on the charges and witnesses they are calling against our client. Remember, you work for Ellie's law firm. That's a fact, we both are listed on their books. And remember, I don't want to be connected with this action, at least not yet. I would like it to be a surprise when we go to court. I want you to feel free to speak up when you have a question or a suggestion." Penny hesitated. "If you have no questions, let's get started."

Penny received a message from the employment agency that they had a woman for her to interview for the secretarial position. She would call to set up a time.

The prospective employee called and Penny set up an interview for late that afternoon. At three sharp, the lady was in the office for the interview. Penny began by asking her name.

She answered, "My name is Josephine, but I prefer to be called Joey."

Penny replied, "Fine, Joey it is. Joey, this job could be temporary. We will be involved in a criminal trial. There is no way of knowing how long it will take—a week, a month, or longer. Have you ever worked for a law firm before?"

Joey replied, "Some time ago, but only for about five months." Anticipating Penny's next question, she added, "The firm finished their job and closed the office. I recently moved here from Seattle and I'm just getting settled in. Three or four months would allow me to become acquainted with the area. I enjoyed working for a law firm."

Penny responded, "We will be a small team: myself, Jimmy, another lawyer, and you. Your job will be more than just secretarial. You will basically be in charge of the office and will be responsible for doing what is required." She couldn't help thinking of her interview with the mother hen. She smiled, it seemed so long ago. "If you want the job, you can start tomorrow."

Joey asked, "What time?"

Penny said, "See you at eight-thirty."

She had a good feeling about Joey.

* * *

Penny was at the sparsely furnished office at 8 a.m.

When Joey walked in, Penny said, "Looks like your first task will be as a decorator. First, let's go meet our neighbors." They went next door and met Harriet, the mother hen.

Harriet told Joey of the office supply stores in the area and gave her the name of the company that put in their computer system. She also told Joey that she could come to her with any request.

Penny joked, "Maybe we just ought to move in here. Well, we had better get moving and make a list of what we need."

The office had three rooms, two large and one smaller. One of the larger rooms would be the receptionist/secretary's office. The other large one would be Penny's office and would be outfitted so it could be used as a conference room. It would have a small conference table, a couple of comfortable chairs, and other pieces of office furniture. The other office would be Jimmy's. Each office would have a computer tied to a network, which allowed all members to interact with each other.

In the main office would be a high speed printer, connected to all the computers. Penny was promised that all would be in and operating by late the next day. That done, it was time to get down to business. Penny got her staff together in the conference room.

She started off, "When we have a conference, it will be with all of us. I want all of us to be fully cognizant of what is going on. I want both of you to express your opinions on anything you think is important. Any questions? No, good. Jimmy, what did you find out?"

Jimmy began, "From the moment I walked in, it was obvious that they were playing this case very close to the vest. They did give me a copy of the indictment and a list of potential witnesses, but no one wanted to talk about the case. When I asked a question, the answer was always, 'I'll have to ask the DA'. It's obviously his ball game.

"The indictment is intentionally vague, just that George is charged with embezzlement and the amount is thirty-seven thousand, three hundred and sixty-seven dollars. The witness list includes the mayor, an auditor, a previous treasurer, and a police captain."

Penny began to outline what she needed. "OK, Joey, I want you to get all the information you can on everyone on the witness list. Google them, check their police records and anything else that comes to mind.

"Jimmy, I want you to check the law on embezzlement. Pay particular attention to what constitutes embezzlement. Does money have to be involved, etcetera. And just so I don't feel left out, I shall talk to my contacts who may know something. Do you all have laptops? I think it would be best if we all have Macs. If you don't, see Joey and she will get you one. Use this office as your base, and I think it would be good if we all meet here at five p.m. to go over what we've learned during the day. OK, good luck and we meet at five," Penny concluded.

* * *

On the day of the trial, Jimmy and Penny arrived early and were seated at the defense table before the DA and his team arrived. The DA was busy with the press and gave little attention to the defense team. He was talking about his campaign to rid the county government of corruption. In the middle of one of his short speeches, the court was called to order.

The judge opened the court with, "Is the prosecutor ready?"

The DA stood up and replied, "Yes, Your Honor."

"Is the defense ready?"

Penny stood up and said, "Yes, Your Honor."

The DA seemed surprised and said, "Your Honor, may I approach the bench?"

The judge nodded and the DA started toward the bench. Penny quickly followed.

The DA sputtered, "This lady can't try this case. She's a member of my staff and would have an unfair advantage."

"Well, Ms. Penny, what say you?" asked the judge.

Penny, speaking a little louder than normal, loud enough that the press could hear, said, "If the DA would have paid as much attention to his office as he has to harassing my client—"

The judge interrupted, "Please, Ms. Penny, just facts."

Penny apologized. "Sorry, Your Honor, but if the DA will check, he will find that I am no longer associated with his office. I resigned two weeks ago. I would think at least he would know who was on his staff."

"Mr. Prosecutor, are you ready for opening statement?" the judge began.

"The prosecution requests a delay of twenty-four hours."

"On what grounds?"

"We need to evaluate what effect Ms. Penny's work in my office will have on this case."

Penny interjected "Objection, Your Honor. I was not associated with any activities involving this case. I was totally occupied in another case for the past three months. The district attorney should be aware of that. The defense desires the trial continues without delay."

The judge proclaimed, "This court will recess for thirty minutes. I will see counsel in my chambers."

In her chambers, it was evident the judge was not happy. "OK, what's going on, Charlie? Don't you really know who's on your staff?"

"Well, I've been very busy preparing for this case," replied the DA.

The judge, a disgusted look on her face, said to the DA, "Then you are prepared. Are you ready to proceed now?"

"Yes, but under protest."

The judge, clearly exasperated, said, "Noted. Now let's go back in and get this done."

Back in the courtroom, with all participants in place and seated, the judge called the court to order and asked the prosecutor if he wanted to make an opening statement. He indicated he did and moved in front of the table, taking a stance like Spencer Tracy playing a southern lawyer.

Penny thought, "If he only had a set of braces for his thumbs, he'd be perfect." She had to control herself to keep from giggling, a very unprofessional thing to do.

The district attorney in an un-Spencer-like voice began. "Ladies and gentlemen of the jury, the prosecution shall prove beyond a shadow of a doubt that Mr. George Appleby, while serving as treasurer for the town of Long Palm, Florida, did intentionally embezzle thirty-nine thousand dollars.

"As district attorney it is my sworn duty to dig out, reveal, and prosecute, to the limit of the law, such crimes. Personally, I feel that to be elected to public office is a great honor, and to violate that trust is despicable and should be punished. I have made that a point of my office. I know you will listen to the evidence and return a verdict of guilty."

Turning to Penny, the judge asked, "Does the defense wish to make an opening statement?"

Penny moved out from the defense table and said, "Yes, Your Honor. The defense will prove that these charges are the result of an overzealous district attorney trumping up these charges to help his reelection campaign and that there was no embezzlement. The district attorney worked with an auditor of his choice who did a questionable audit, his only purpose being to find evidence of embezzlement. Because of an inaccurate, nay, a careless audit, they found what they claim was an embezzlement just to prove the DA was rooting out corruption. It looks like he may have started in the wrong office. I'm sure when we present our case, you will find our client innocent and wronged for political reasons. Thank you, Your Honor." She sat down.

"The prosecution may call its first witness."

"The prosecution calls Mayor Green."

The mayor took the stand and was sworn in, and the prosecution begins its questioning.

"Mr. Mayor. You are the mayor of Long Palm, Florida?"

"I am. I'm in my second year as mayor."

"How did the embezzlement come to your attention?"

"I received a tip that there was an irregularity in our treasurer's books."

"What action did you take?"

"I hired an accountant to audit the treasurer's books."

"And what did he find?"

"He found a large sum missing that could not be accounted for in the audit."

"No further questions."

The judge said, "Your witness, Ms. Penny."

Penny rose and asked, "Mr. Mayor. From whom did you receive the tip that initiated this investigation?"

"I would rather not say."

"I would rather you did. It will help us get to the root of this. You do want to find out if there really was an embezzlement?"

The mayor, a little agitated, mumbled, "Certainly, that's why I hired the auditor."

"The question is still, why did you think you needed to have an audit?"

"It was in a discussion with the district attorney."

Penny said, "The DA? What was the occasion and how did it come up?"

"It was at one of the DA's fundraising events. The DA was talking about what he wanted to do about corruption in government. I asked him how he was going to start. He said there were usually a number of rumors about shady deals, and he would start looking at those. In fact, he said he had heard something about my treasurer. I was surprised, I told him our treasurer had been in office for years, and I have never heard anything derogatory about him. The DA said, 'Those are the ones you have to watch, maybe you ought to check. Do a quick, quiet audit. No one will know. If nothing is found, no one is hurt. If something is found, the suspect won't be put on guard.' He said if I wanted to check, he could recommend a really good, discreet auditor, Mr. Hopkins, who is a specialist in uncovering corruption in public service and can do an audit and no one will have to know. He said, think about it."

"So you ordered an audit?" Penny asked

"I didn't on my own. The city council had a meeting and decided to have an audit."

"Did you authorize the audit?"

"With the approval of the city council."

"Was this in a regular meeting?"

"No, we just got together."

"Is that normal? Is it legal?"

"No, it's not normal, but it's legal in an emergency."

"How many members were present?"

"Sufficient for a quorum."

"Did this emergency meeting happened before or after Mr. Appleby went on his cruise?"

"The DA told me before Mr. Appleby took his vacation. The meeting was called after he was gone."

"Don't you think it would have been more fair and more productive if he was there?"

"The DA said we shouldn't give him notice as he might alter the books."

"So you gave Mr. Hopkins a contract, and what did he find?"

"He did an audit and said there was a thirty-nine thousand dollar deficit."

"Did you take any steps to verify his findings?"

"No, he was highly recommended by the DA."

"No further questions," concluded Penny.

Turning to the prosecution, the judge said, "You may call your next witness."

"We call Mr. Hopkins," the prosecution responded. "Mr. Hopkins, what are your qualifications as an auditor?

The auditor began, "I have a degree in accounting from the University of Florida and I am a CPA. I worked for a major accounting office for eight years before I started my own firm."

"Do you have a specialization?"

"Yes. Although my firm does all kinds of accounting work, I specialize in public mismanagement."

"Have you done many such investigations?"

"We completed seven in the past four years."

"And your findings?"

"We found four discrepancies that were subject to prosecution. We turned our findings over to the authorities."

"And on this present case, how did this come about?"

"I received a call from the mayor asking me to do an audit of his treasurer's books. He said he'd received a tip that there may be problems."

"And what did you find?"

"In the audit we found that thirty-nine thousand dollars was unaccounted for. We turned all the information over to your office."

"No further questions. Your witness," the prosecution said to Penny.

She began, "How did you get involved in the previous cases, Mr. Hopkins?"

"We would receive a request from a government official in charge, a mayor, a commissioner, or a department head, someone in charge."

"Of the four problems you found and turned over for prosecution, how many convictions were there?"

"Two. I believe the others are still in the court system."

"Two out of seven. Not an impressive record, is it?"

"Objection. Mr. Hopkins's record is not the subject of the court," the prosecution injected.

The judge responded, "Objection sustained. The defense will confine her questions to the subject at hand."

Penny continued, "Sorry, Your Honor. I'm a baseball fan, two out of seven won't get you in the Hall of Fame."

"Ms. Penny, next question please," interrupted the judge.

"How comprehensive was your audit?"

"Sufficient to find a problem."

"Was that the purpose of the audit, to find a problem?"

"If a problem existed, yes, it was our job to find and report it."

"Was a one hundred thousand dollar donation part of the problem?"

"Yes, I believe it was involved."

"So you didn't check to see how long this problem had existed?"

"No, we performed an audit as requested." Hopkins was obviously showing some discomfort.

Penny turned her attention to the judge and asked, "May I approach the bench?"

"Please," she responded.

Penny and the DA went in front of the judge. She said, "Your Honor. If I might call my client to the stand, we can clear up this case right now.

The DA noted, "This is highly irregular. But if she calls her client, I have the right to reexamine."

"Fine with me," said Penny.

The judge nodded. "Call your witness."

"I call Mr. Appleby to the stand."

After he was sworn in, Penny began the questioning. "Mr. Appleby, are you aware of any incident that may affect the city's accounts?"

"Yes, it happened thirty years ago."

"Please explain."

Mr. Appleby began, "Thirty years ago, the wealthy owner of a hardware store set up a trust, valued at one hundred thousand dollars. The provision was the city would use one thousand dollars a month to maintain the park on the main street. They would take the money from the trust's earnings, figuring that amount would never exceed the earnings.

"It didn't for nearly six years, but then the market changed, and the trust began to lose money. But the city continued to take a thousand dollars a month, resulting in the trust diminishing. When it got to sixty-one thousand dollars, the city council decided to transfer the maintenance of the park to the city parks department and see if the trust could replenish itself. For some reason, they decided to maintain the donor's honor by showing the total amount of the gift of one hundred thousand dollars on the books, and to make an allowance for any discrepancy. It was a decision of the city council, over the objection of the city treasurer. Over the years, it became a part of the system and it was until now."

"Would an audit show this as a discrepancy?" Penny continued.

"Yes. Unless the auditor made an effort to check with previous audits, he would come to this conclusion."

"Would the mayor be aware of this?"

"He should be, although he has been in office less than four years. Time of the last audit."

"Then in your opinion as a long-time treasurer, was there a real shortage in the treasurer's books?"

"No, just some nonsense put in the books a number of years ago by some well-meaning politicians," said the treasurer.

Penny finished questioning her client.

"Does the prosecutor have any questions?" asked the judge.

The prosecutor responded, "Yes, Your Honor. Mr. Appleby, did you tell the mayor or any other official about this?"

"I tried to tell the mayor and I tried to tell you. Neither of you were interested and refused to listen."

"I don't remember not listening," stated the DA.

"Objection, Your Honor, "Penny said. "If the DA wants to testify, let him be sworn in and take the stand. I'll be glad to question him."

"Objection sustained, the rest is unnecessary," the judge replied.

"Sorry, Your Honor," Penny said with a smile. The judge tried to stay stern, but a smile slipped across her face.

"Your next question," the judge said to the DA.

"No further questions, Your Honor," he concluded.

"The court will recess for forty-five minutes. Counsel in my chambers," the judge told the courtroom.

When all participants were seated, the judge, who appeared very annoyed, said, "Who wants to explain this mess?"

They all looked at the DA, who was squirming in his seat. The DA began, "I was only doing what my office is supposed to. I was prosecuting a crime."

Penny jumped in. "A nonexistent crime that you perpetuated for political reasons. Now that it's been exposed, I think the case should be thrown out and an apology made to Mr. Appleby. As Mr. Appleby's lawyer, I can't see any reason why I shouldn't recommend that he sues the city council, the mayor, the district attorney, and the auditor for defamation of character, slander, and a couple of other charges I'll come up with."

The mayor said, "Wait a minute. I just followed a suggestion by the DA."

The judge raised her hand to stop all the talking and addressed the DA. "Let's take one thing at a time. First, was there an embezzlement, Charlie?"

"I'm not sure. If what Mr. Appleby says is true, then no, there were no missing funds," he answered.

"How do we check for the truth, Penny?" the judge asked.

"There are still several members of the city council around. Call and ask them. That's what should have been done before they started this."

The judge said, "This is what we are going to do. Tomorrow, without the jury, we will convene in my courtroom, with all the participants and the entire city council. If any council member verifies that what Mr. Appleby said is true, the case against him will be dismissed. After that, it will be up to Mr. Appleby and his lawyer what comes next. I will see all of you in my court, tomorrow at ten a.m. sharp."

The next day at 10 a.m., the judge called her court to order. She began, "This will be a question and answer session. I will ask the questions and some you will supply the answers. You will be sworn in and be liable for perjury. I first call the district attorney."

He was sworn in and took the stand.

"You were the first to suggest that there might be a problem in the treasurer's books. How did you arrive at that?" asked the judge.

"Your Honor, my office receives many tips on possible crimes. I scan them and a member of my staff decides if they are worthy of investigation and to which department the tip should go. When I was with the mayor, I remembered that one of the tips was about his treasurer and I told him. He took it from there."

The judge turned to Penny. "Ms. Penny do you have any questions?"

"Thank you, Your Honor. When you passed that tip to your staff, what did they do with it?"

"I'm afraid I didn't follow up on that," responded the DA.

"Wouldn't you think if there was a problem, your staff would have found an anomaly?"

"I'm not sure how far their investigation went."

"So this whole affair started on an unverified tip?"

"Your Honor, I thought this session was supposed to determine if an embezzlement took place. Let's get to questioning those that have information on that."

"Yes, let us do that," replied the judge. "I call, Mr. James Gross."

Mr. Gross took the stand and was sworn in, and the judge asked the first question. "Are you a member of the city council?

"Yes, I have been a member for nine years."

"Are you aware of the one hundred thousand dollar gift made many years ago and how it's been handled in the budget?"

"Yes, it has come up over the years. The treasurer wanted it changed, but there were members who didn't. The council members always won. They did something that eliminated it as a problem. So over the years we just ignored it."

"Thank you," said the judge. "Next I call Mrs. Helen Clark."

Mrs. Clark took the stand, was sworn in.

"You are a member of the city council?" she asked.

"Yes, I have been for thirteen years," replied Mrs. Clark.

"Then you are familiar with that part of the budget under discussion?"

"Oh, yes. It was one my ancestors that made the donation. It was my father who insisted that the original amount be declared in the budget. The treasurer at the time opposed it, but came up with a 'fix' that allowed it to be in the budget without messing up the final audit. They kept trying to change it, but we've been able to keep it as is. The trust is starting to come back and it is estimated that in the next thirteen years it will be back to the original one hundred thousand dollars. Then the trust will read that only the yearly earning will be used for the park."

"Mr. District Attorney, do you still want to pursue this case?" interrupted the judge.

"No, Your Honor," he responded. "The prosecution recommends the charges against Mr. Appleby be dismissed."

"Ms. Penny, do you have anything to say?" said the judge.

"Just that we are thankful that this travesty has been rectified."

"All charges against Mr. Appleby are dismissed. This court is adjourned," the judge declared with a strike of the gavel.

Outside the courthouse, Penny ran into a horde of press. This would be her chance to make a pitch for Max.

"Ms. O'Dowd, you made some harsh remarks about the DA in your opening remarks. Do you stand by those accusations?" a reporter shouted.

"It is my opinion that the district attorney is incompetent and, as you saw in the trial today, more interested in keeping his job than in dispensing justice," said Penny. "It is for those reasons that I resigned and I am giving my full support to help elect Maxine Witte to be our next district attorney."

EPILOGUE

D r. Sam was talking with Suzy about nothing in particular when out of the blue she asked, "Would you like to have a baby?"

Suzy couldn't find anything to say except "Where did that come from?" It finally came out: "Yes."

"It surprised me too. I just remembered looking at a paper I received from a sperm bank, which I've had occasion to use for some of my patients. I totally forgot I had placed some of Timmy's sperm there. It was a spur of the moment decision, almost an afterthought. I was sending another patient's sample, and I thought, why not? And I forgot about it until I got an invoice from the bank.

"The thing is, if you and Penny want a child, you can probably be a mother," said Dr. Sam.

Suzy was still in shock and still trying to digest what she had just heard. "Have you told Penny?"

"No. As I told you, I just realized the possibilities. Maybe we could even have a wedding," continued Dr. Sam.

"Whoa," said Suzy. "You're moving too fast for me. Maybe we should have a board meeting to discuss this."

"A board meeting? Yes, interested parties, MaryAnne, Kathy, Max, Ellie, Harriet, David, and of course Penny, why not, let's make it a party at my place," replied Dr. Sam.

Suzy was getting excited. "Fine. Let's keep it a secret until then."

"OK, we'll have it this weekend."

"You really think I could be a mother?" asked Suzy.

Dr. Sam responded, "Happens every day!"

The next day, all "members of the board" received an invitation to a meeting at Dr. Sam's: *The dress is casual and attendance is mandatory. Everyone's presence will be noted, and a vote will be taken!*

Everyone was calling, trying to find out: What? No one would admit to knowing anything. Even Sam, at whose house the meeting was to be held, admitted nothing, except when Suzy called her. No one wanted to miss whatever it was, so they would all be there.

On Saturday evening, they started arriving early. Suzy was there first, helping Sam set up a bar and put out snacks. David came into the living room, made himself a drink, and went to his favorite chair and sat down. He thought, "This should be interesting, and if I'm smart, I'll stay on the outside and look in."

Ellie and Harriet arrived next, and although full of curiosity said nothing. Suzy gave each of them a drink and let them choose a seat.

Max was next, and she was not quiet. "OK, what's this all about?"

No one answered. Ellie finally said, "We're all in the dark. Maybe Penny knows."

MaryAnne and Penny arrived at the same time. They all looked expectantly at Penny. "What?" was her only remark.

Suzy came into the room. "If you all will get a drink and find a chair, this meeting will come to order."

There was a low murmur and then total silence as Sam raised her voice. "This meeting is to help two dear friends make a decision that will affect all of us."

There was tension in the air as Sam continued. "The question is"—she hesitated—"should Penny and Suzy have a baby?"

There was a mixture of expressions: gasp, chuckles, and some of relief, for who knew what might have been the problem.

Penny was in a daze. "What are you talking about?"

Sam began, "If you all will stay seated, I will explain."

She did, and when finished, she turned to Penny and asked, "What do you think?"

"If Suzy thinks it's a good idea, then I'm all for it," Penny exclaimed.

Suzy rushed over and gave Penny a big hug. There were hugs all round.

David, who had been sitting quietly in his chair, thought, "What the hell? I'm not smart. I might as well get in the middle." He stood up and announced, "If they are going to have a baby, then they should get married."

That brought a hush to the festivities. Max asked, "How can that be?"

"Why, I took him from Tim to Penny. I can take him back to Tim long enough to get married, said Dr. Sam. "I even can get a priest to perform the ceremony."

Suzy exclaimed, "It's a good thing you went with the FBI, you would have made one hell of a master criminal."

There was a lot of talk, even as far as someone suggesting baby names.

Sam finally said, "I think we've done everything we can tonight. Let's all go home and sleep on it. We'll get together later."

As they left, they all stopped to give Suzy and Penny hugs. Penny and Suzy went to the condo and spent most of the night talking. Both were excited about the prospect of being parents, Penny to continue the Thomas name, Suzy to be a mother. They decided to invite everyone down to the beach for the weekend.

Suzy changed the sign to "OPTIONAL." Mars and Pax were there to greet everyone, checking each female for beach bags that might have a stray bra inside.

They all made their way to the beach. Suzy and Penny, who always went topless at the beach, immediately removed their tops. The rest followed. David, who had become adjusted to being on the beach with a bunch of topless women, didn't bat an eye. All the ladies made sure their discarded tops were safe inside a zippered bag.

The pups roved around looking for something to get into. Penny took out a couple of tennis balls and threw them down the beach. Mars and Pax took off and grabbed them and brought them back to whoever was willing to play. They continued until they tired out. Then then came back and lay down beside Suzy with their tongues hanging out.

Penny related their experience with the two young men and how the dogs reacted.

David spoke up. "I think it would be a good idea for Suzy to go to her parents in Maine, where she can meet Timmy and start a relationship. After a couple of weeks, she can come back, and when Timmy decides to take a job in South America, they decide they want to get married before he goes. We will have a proxy marriage here with Penny standing in as the proxy. The priest will perform the ceremony, not knowing he is actually marrying them."

Suzy spoke up. "Devious, but I like it. My parents have been asking when I was going to visit. I can leave this weekend."

Sam said, "When you get back, I'll book you into the Family Center in Winter Park, they are the best in Florida for this procedure."

Suzy remarked, "Someone has to watch the pups, since they seem to be attached to Max."

Max jumped up. "Whoa, I've run out of lingerie with those two perverts." Everyone was laughing.

Penny chimed in, "Don't worry, I'll move down and take care of these two. I have a number of old bras. Guess that takes care of everything for now. Let's enjoy the rest of the day."

After a couple of weeks, Suzy returned and checked into the Family Center, and when they were sure the procedure had been successful, they made the arrangements for the wedding.

They decided to have the ceremony at the chapel at their church. Father O'Connor would preside. David was the best man and Dr. Sam was the bride's maid.

Father O'Connor explained that this was a proxy ceremony and Penny, acting as a proxy, would answer for Timothy.

She said "I do" in the appropriate places and after Father O'Connor pronounced them husband and wife, David produced a marriage license, previously signed by Penny as Timothy N. Thomas. When it was signed by Suzy, they were legally married.

The champagne flowed and the party lasted past midnight. Penny and Suzy drove down to the beach house to start their married life and to await the birth of their baby.

BABY

After Max won the election and became the new DA, Penny continued to maintain her office at Ellie's. She was always available to represent any police officer in trouble or any deserving soul who lacked the funds needed for a good lawyer.

As often happens with these pregnancies, Suzy became a mother of two, one of each. A great start for the next generation of Thomases.

The female offspring was named Erin Elizabeth after her parents' mothers, and the male was named Timothy Terrance Thomas, continuing the long line of Terrys and Timmys.

It was when Suzy was in her eighth month that Penny was talking with Dr. Sam and told her that some doctor friend (MaryAnne) had told Suzy that a male could produce milk if his breasts were massaged enough.

"Suzy has begun massaging my breasts every night, but nothing has happened yet," Penny said.

"If it bothers you, tell her to quit," said Dr. Sam.

"Are you kidding? I love it," responded Penny.

…….But can it work?

THE END